Hogan, Ray

The rawhiders

D587 11.95

THE RAWHIDERS

THE RAWHIDERS

RAY HOGAN

DOUBLEDAY & COMPANY, INC.
GARDEN CITY, NEW YORK
1985

All of the characters in this book
are fictitious, and any resemblance
to actual persons, living or dead,
is purely coincidental.

Library of Congress Cataloging in Publication Data

Hogan, Ray, 1908–
The rawhiders.

I. Title.
PS3558.03473R35   1985   813'.54
ISBN: 0-385-19998-8
Library of Congress Catalog Card Number 84-24671
Copyright © 1985 by Ray Hogan
ALL RIGHTS RESERVED
PRINTED IN THE UNITED STATES OF AMERICA
FIRST EDITION

To my wife,
LOIS CLAYTON HOGAN

THE RAWHIDERS

1

Matt Buckman heard the renegade Kiowas before he saw them. Midway across a narrow, flinty mesa, with the volcanic formation known as Capulin Mountain well behind him, he suddenly found himself trapped in the open with the braves, yelling and shooting, bearing down on him in a two-pronged charge.

Raking the bay gelding he was riding with his spurs and sending the big horse surging forward, Buckman drew his rifle from its boot and glanced hurriedly about for the nearest cover. He could never make a stand where he was; there were at least a dozen of the Kiowas in the party, all outcasts from their tribe, according to information he'd received from a rancher who had warned him of the probability of his encountering them.

Not far on ahead was a scatter of small, rocky hills. None appeared large enough or sufficiently covered with brush to provide much in the way of protection, but they were his only chance. Bending low in the saddle, the bloodcurdling yells of the renegades filling his ears, Matt rode hard for the hillocks.

The likelihood of coming up against a party of hostile Indians had been far from Matt Buckman's

mind when he'd ridden out of Taos a few days earlier with Dodge City as his destination. It was to be
the beginning of a lark—a vacation. He'd spent that
past year working for Charlie Able on the C-A
Ranch which lay in the shadow of nearby Cerro
Vista Peak, and now, with what he'd saved of his
wages in a money belt around his middle, he was off
to see the elephant and, hopefully, sign on with
some rancher shipping a herd from Dodge to Chicago.

That had been a longtime dream of Matt's, riding
a string of cattle cars loaded with steers destined for
market in Chicago. He'd heard talk of the town, of
how big it was, of what-all a man could see and do
there: thus one day that previous winter as he was
hazing a jag of cattle from one snowy pasture to
another he made up his mind: as soon as spring
roundup was over and Charlie Able had no need for
him, he'd do just that.

If he was lucky he'd get to sign on with a herd
being shipped east, but if that didn't develop, he
reckoned he had enough cash in his belt to pay his
fare there and back, eat, and maybe even set in on a
card game or two.

A bullet caromed off the horn of his saddle and
whistled off into the hot, still air. The yelling of the
Kiowas seemed louder, nearer. Matt threw a hasty
glance over his left shoulder, and then the right.
The two streaming columns of half-clad braves were
gaining on him. But the first knoll, while not the
largest, was just ahead. He'd make it if—

Abruptly the bay stumbled, went to his knees—hit
by a Kiowa bullet or from stepping into a gopher

hole. Matt, cursing his luck, came down on hands and knees. He heard the crack of wood as the stock of his rifle broke free of the metal. Releasing his grip on the now useless weapon, Matt drew the .45 he carried on his hip and, lunging to his feet, legged it for the safety of the hill.

He reached the brush and plunged into it with the screeching of the braves and the hammering of their rifles filling the air. A tub-size black rock next to which a stunted juniper struggled to maintain life lay near the center of the mound. Other, smaller chunks of lava, a few needle-sharp yuccas, and shin-high yellowed grass covered the rise. Throwing himself in close to the juniper, Buckman went full length onto his belly, and cocking the .45 snapped a bullet at the nearest of the oncoming renegades.

It was a lucky shot. The heavy slug caught the brave in the chest. He stiffened on the pony he was riding, a look of surprise covering his dark, glistening face, and then as bloodstains began to spread rapidly across the front of the deerskin shirt he was wearing, he tipped to one side and fell to the ground.

Immediately the rest of the Kiowas slowed and began to pull away. Taking advantage of the moment Matt flipped open the loading gate of his pistol and not only replaced the spent cartridge but filled as well the empty chamber in the cylinder that he always left empty in the interest of safety. He'd need every bullet he had if he was to hold off the Kiowas, Matt thought, and then swore grimly. There was damn little chance of him being able to do that.

His horse was back up on its feet and being led away, Buckman saw. Evidently the big gelding had just tripped and not been hurt. He was glad the bay had not been killed. He'd owned and ridden him for the past three years, and he was a good horse, but he reckoned he was seeing the last of the gelding now.

Raising his head slightly Matt watched the braves draw together and halt. Staying well out of pistol range, they began to go through his saddlebags and blanket roll. Some of the articles they cast aside indifferently, others they claimed. His saddle was discarded; such placed too much unnecessary weight on a horse, causing it to tire quickly and slow down, Indians believed, and Matt reckoned it was true.

Working his way into the space between the lava rock and the juniper Matt pulled off his hat, brushed at the sweat on his forehead, and settled in for a last-ditch fight. In his mid-twenties, Buckman was a lean, spare man with dark hair and eyes and a blunt jaw. Wearing ordinary range clothing—heavy shirt, tan duck pants, boots with built-up heels, neckerchief, leather vest, and a sun-faded brown hat crimped and creased to contend with the weather, whatever it might be—he looked no different from the dozens of other cowboys who rode across the area or worked the ranges of the ranches in that upper part of New Mexico Territory.

The Kiowas, with much bickering and scuffling, had finished their ransacking of his possessions and were now vaulting back onto their ponies. One, a thin, wiry brave with a necklace of what looked to be turkey feathers, appeared to be the leader of the party. Motioning at the others to stay where they were he rode forward, moving directly toward Matt.

The Indian was not just demonstrating his bravery to the remaining Kiowas, Buckman guessed, but was testing him. Turkey Feather, as Matt figured he was probably called, wanted to see how near he could get without drawing fire, after which he would have an idea of the range of Matt's weapon.

Buckman waited until the brave was within reach of his .45 and then deliberately fired low. The bullet kicked up sand several feet short of the Kiowa. Matt grinned in satisfaction as the renegade halted. He could have let the brave draw closer and knocked him off his horse with an easy shot. But Turkey Feather counted for only one in the party of renegades; better to play it smart, arrange it so the braves would misjudge what they considered a safe distance from him, and, when they rode in close, unload on several of them.

Rodding out the spent cartridge, Matt thumbed in a fresh one and watched the brave. Turkey Feather seemed to study the situation for a full minute as if deciding what to do next, and then abruptly he raised his fist overhead and, giving forth a series of rapid, discordant yells, wheeled and rejoined the other Indians.

A discussion of some sort followed his return. It broke up after a few moments, and then the party split into halves again and rode off slowly into opposite directions. That they planned to come at him again from both sides was clear to Matt.

Reaching down he unbuckled his gun belt and

laid it out alongside him, quickly counting the brass cartridges as he did. Fourteen shells—plus the six in the gun itself. There was a full box in his saddle-bags, along with a supply for his rifle, but neither would do him any good now. The brave who had claimed the bay gelding had taken over the leather pouches and probably possessed their contents, and the rifle lay broken into two pieces out where the gelding had tripped and gone down.

Matt glanced up at the sky as he again mopped at the sweat on his face. It was a clean, cloudless blue from which the unimpeded sun blazed down with a steady fierceness. It was hot for early summer, he thought, and he shrugged. Being pinned down as he was on the hill could make it seem that way.

The horse of the dead brave had drifted off to-ward the bay, now tethered to a clump of brush on the far side of the flat. The pony seemed uncertain whether to follow the Kiowa party as they rode off or stay with the gelding. After a bit it decided on the latter course and continued on to where the gelding was standing. Halting, it began to graze on the thin grass and dried weeds that hugged the ground.

Matt considered his chances of leaving the safety of the hill and making a run for his horse. He just might catch the Kiowas off guard and reach the gelding before they realized what was happening. But then what? He'd be out in the open again, and in no time at all they would run him down. No, it was better he stay put, fight it out from the hill—and hope for a miracle.

Shifting about in the uncomfortable heat Matt watched as the two parties of braves came to a stop, one to the north of him, the other to the south. After a moment he shook his head. It wasn't going to stop with that; three braves had pulled away from the others and were heading for a point somewhere in between. They would be coming at him from three directions.

A hard grin again split Buckman's dry lips. He reckoned this would be it. He'd be going under now —no doubt about it—but he sure as hell would be taking a few of those red devils with him! He was a damn good shot with his .45, and just as soon as the renegades made their charge and got within range he'd finish off two or three. Maybe that would turn them back once more when they saw he wasn't about to just throw in his cards and quit.

Hell, they just might even forget about him and go on! They already had what they wanted—his horse. The rifle would be a prize, too, but they no doubt saw that it was broken and of no use. As for his pistol—

A sudden burst of yells brought Buckman up short. The renegades were on the move. They were coming straight for him from three sides, yelling, brandishing their rifles or the metal-tipped lances that some carried as a weapon overhead as they rushed across the flat in the bright sunlight.

Taut, Matt flattened out in the space between the lava rock and the stunted juniper, striving to make of himself as small a target as possible. He'd stay calm, bide his time, and down the nearest brave first —probably one of those racing in from the center group, which appeared to be slightly ahead of the others. After that it would be a matter of turning fast, either left or right, to meet the closest brave.

But Matt Buckman was not fooling himself. He had about as much chance of coming out of this shoot-out with the Kiowa renegades as he had of catching wind in a net. He'd not just give in, though; he'd give one hell of an account of himself before it was over.

Stretched out on his belly, hat tipped forward to shade his eyes, pistol firm in his two hands, Buckman leveled the weapon at the brave in the forefront of the oncoming Kiowas. Waiting until the renegade was within range, he triggered a shot.

2

As the weapon bucked in his hands, Matt watched the brave in the lead of the party jolt, throw up his hands, and fall from his horse. Wasting no time Buckman swung to his right. The renegade coming at him from that side was so close Matt could see the gleam of his bared teeth, the wild look in his eyes. Buckman fired fast. The Kiowa clutched at his belly, buckled forward, and throwing his arms about the neck of his pony to prevent falling, veered off.

Bullets were digging into the weedy soil around Matt, slamming into the rocks, and clipping through the thin needles of the juniper. Dust and powder smoke were beginning to hang over the hill, and the yells of the Kiowas had become much louder and more nerve-racking. A lance stabbed into the ground an arm's length from where Matt lay and stood quivering upright in the hot sunlight.

Triggering his pistol again at one of the braves on his right, and missing, Buckman twisted about, sent a bullet racing for a Kiowa renegade, off his pony and rushing in on him from that side. The man went down as the lead smashed into his chest and drove him backward.

The Indians were all around the hill riding in a diminishing circle, firing at will and with little direction other than in the general direction of where he lay. Conscious of his dwindling supply of ammunition, Matt took careful aim and dropped another of the braves. A burst of yells went up at that. A second lance thudded into the dry soil of the hill, and the shooting increased. Grim, Buckman hurriedly reloaded and prepared himself for a concerted rush by the braves which was certain to come soon.

They would get nothing but satisfaction from killing him, he thought. His rifle was broken, and they already had his horse as well as his gear. Of course they'd take his pistol and gun belt but they would serve for trading purposes only; braves didn't care for handguns, finding them much too difficult to shoot accurately and of no use at all for hunting.

The band of renegades had been preying on pilgrims moving along the trail west for the past several weeks, Matt had been told. Usually they killed the men and took what they wanted from the contents of the wagon. At times they molested the women and they almost always took the horses. So far the army and lawmen in the area had been unable to put a stop to the depredation. The renegades kept on the move constantly and could be counted on to never remain in one place for any length of time.

Another lance thudded into the sun-baked ground beyond the juniper. It was followed by a flurry of bullets, one of which notched the brim of Buckman's hat. Matt set himself. This would be the beginning of another run at him, he reckoned—perhaps the last.

The dry rustle of dead grass and weeds nearby

sent a surge of alarm through him. Instinctively he rolled to one side. The sweaty, glistening copper figure of a brave—eyes narrowed, mouth open in a wild yell, hand clutching a long-bladed knife—was lunging for him.

Matt fired instantly at point-blank range. The heavy bullet drove into the Kiowa's chest. The brave's head snapped back as his body seemed to freeze in motion. The knife fell from his nerveless fingers, and, mouth still flared but emitting no sound, he hung there upright for a long moment and then collapsed.

Matt turned his attention quickly back to the remaining Kiowas. They were still riding back and forth but there was less shooting. They seemed to be hesitating, actually pulling away for some reason. In the next bit of time Buckman heard other gunshots. They came from nearby, and a different direction. Cautious, Matt raised his head to have a look. Three riders closely followed by a canvastopped wagon, pulled by a strong team, were bearing down on him from a grove of trees on to the east.

Turkey Feather and his renegades had drawn together into a single group and were milling about, seemingly uncertain what to do, or perhaps were uniting to meet the oncoming riders and the wagon. But one thing was certain in Matt Buckman's mind: the newcomers meant his salvation! Evidently they had heard the gunfire, investigated, and seen that he was a doomed man unless helped.

A shout broke out from the suddenly quiet Indians. Turkey Feather raised his rifle above his head, shook it vigorously, and gave forth a string of yells. Drumming his heels against the flanks of his pony he sent the horse racing toward the three men and the wagon, hopeful of cutting them off before they could reach the island of brush and rock where Buckman was making his desperate stand. Immediately the rest of the Kiowas, echoing their chief's wild, quavering notes, followed.

The riders and the driver of the wagon never slackened their speed, but came on. Matt, snatching up his gun belt and strapping it on, drew himself fully upright. Triggering a couple of shots at the Kiowas, he moved to the edge of the brush and faced the oncoming wagon, now veering toward him.

"Get aboard!" the driver yelled, slowing as he drew in close. He had his rifle out, was now using it.

Matt spurted away from the brush and ran for the canvas-topped vehicle as it momentarily slowed. The riders, in between the wagon and the renegades, had opened up on the braves in an apparent attempt to turn them back, or at least slow them, but their shots were having little effect on the Kiowas as they continued their headlong approach.

"Come on—come on!" the driver of the wagon, a large, yellow-bearded man, shouted.

Buckman was in no need of urging. He was reaching for the tail gate of the vehicle when he heard the man's strident voice. Taking a firm grip on the thick cross board as the wagon began to gather speed, Matt hooked his body over the gate. For several moments he was precariously balanced, half in, half out of the rocking, jolting vehicle, and then with a final heave he launched himself into the bed.

The stench of drying hides assailed his nostrils. Rawhiders! He had been rescued from the Kiowas by a party of hide hunters—but there was no time to think about that. Drawing his pistol he moved to the end of the wagon. Two of the riders had swung in behind, and were not far back. They were shooting over their shoulders at the Indians. The third man was a dark blur on the flat; his riderless horse, wild with fright, was keeping pace with the wagon a hundred yards or so off to the side. Matt whirled to the driver.

"One of your bunch has been hit!" he yelled above the clatter and pounding of the swaying vehicle.

The yellow-bearded man turned, glanced back. He swore loudly.

"Penmon—the damned fool! Might've known he'd get himself shot!"

Matt braced himself for a sudden change in course. It didn't come. Reloading his empty pistol he shouted again at the rawhider. "Ain't you going back after him? Could be he's not dead—"

"He's dead all right," the yellow-bearded man stated flatly. "If he ain't right now he mighty soon will be. Them Indians don't waste no time on a white man."

Buckman, finished with loading his weapon, stared at the driver. From what he could see the man was large, undeniably powerful, with thick arms, wide shoulders, and an almost invisible neck. He would be somewhere in his forties, Matt guessed, and had a leathery face, small black eyes under thick brows, a matted, dirty beard, and an equally unkempt mustache.

His clothing—black, greasy pants, red shirt with dirty underwear sleeves showing below the elbows, stained, lead-colored, uncreased hat, and a vest that was much too small for his thick torso—was filthy and no doubt smelled as bad as the horse and cattle hides covering the wagon bed.

"Do some shooting, damn it!" he yelled, suddenly aware that Matt had finished reloading and was staring at him. "Help them boys some or we'll all be a-laying out there on the flat for them renegades to carve up."

Buckman turned about, braced himself against the wagon's tailgate, and began to fire at the Kiowas.

"You ain't going to do no good with that pistol," the rawhider yelled. "Best you use this," he added, and as Matt looked around tossed him the rifle that he had laid on the floorboards.

Buckman caught the weapon, slid the six-gun back into its holster, and, jacking a cartridge into the rifle's chamber, took aim through the haze of trailing dust at one of the renegades. Pressing off the shot, he grunted in satisfaction. He was not familiar with the weapon, but the sights were true. The brave had stiffened on his pony and immediately swung off. Levering a fresh cartridge into place Matt lined up on another of the renegades and triggered a second shot. It was a miss but the bullet had apparently grazed the brave as he slowed his pony and began to drop back.

Bracing himself as best he could against the jolting of the wagon, ignoring the sickening smell of the hides, Matt leveled the rifle at a third brave, being careful to keep his line of fire well clear of the two riders, now racing along behind and slightly to one side of the vehicle.

Waiting until the wagon settled down after bounding over a rock or some other obstruction in its path, Buckman triggered the weapon. The brave he had targeted instantly crumpled on his pony and fell to the ground.

Immediately the remainder of the renegade party, now much smaller in number than it had been at the start, began to pull up. Matt caught a glimpse of Turkey Feather, rifle raised above his head, not in a gesture of attack as it had been earlier, but now signaling to break off and withdraw.

"Beat them off—that's what we done!" the driver of the wagon shouted jubilantly. "Yes, sir, we sure did! That was some mighty fine shooting, mister. I'm Cud Hooker. Come on up here and tell me what folks call you."

The wagon had slowed and was now veering toward a stand of trees off to the left. Buckman, rifle in hand, crawled over the pile of hides to the front of the vehicle and up onto the seat beside Hooker. The man, he learned quickly, smelled every bit as bad as the load of hides he was carrying.

"Name's Matt Buckman," he said, laying the rifle on the floor. "I'm mighty obliged to you for getting me out of that fight. Figured my cashing-in time had come for sure."

"Well, Indians are something I ain't never had no

use for," Hooker drawled as the horses fell back into an easy trot. "Weren't about to leave you there for them to carve up; couldn't leave nobody in a fix like that, in fact." The rawhider paused, motioned to one of the two riders who had ridden in close. "Rooster, you best go round up Penmon's horse. We'll meet you in the grove."

The rider addressed as Rooster, a slim, blond, pale-eyed man wearing an old army campaign hat along with other articles of clothing reminiscent of the conflict between the states, nodded in understanding and, cutting away, rode to get the dead rawhider's horse, which was now following the wagon.

"Can shake hands with Rooster and Fargo when we make camp," Hooker said. "Seeing the kind of shooter you are, I expect they'll cotton to you real good."

3

Hooker drove the team and wagon into the grove he had indicated and pulled to a stop alongside a small creek, one no wider than the length of a man's arm or deeper than a hand's width. Rooster arrived at almost the same time leading Penmon's horse by its reins. Fargo, the other rawhider, was there ahead of them all, hunched over the stream slaking his thirst. He drew himself upright and turned to Hooker.

"We camping here?" he asked in a deep, raspy voice.

A large, dark man with a broad, heavily lined, bearded face and shoe-button eyes, he was equal to Cud Hooker in size and probably in strength. He was wearing a stained yellow shirt, greasy denim pants, scarred knee-high boots, a wide-brimmed flat-crowned hat, and a tweed vest across the front of which a fancy gold watch chain hung in a short loop.

"Reckon it's as good a place as any," Hooker replied as he and Matt came down off the wagon. The rawhider bucked his head at Matt. "This here fellow's handle is Buckman. Expect you both got a good look-see at how handy he is with a rifle. . . . Buckman, meet one of my partners there, name's Fargo Smith."

Fargo extended a big hand to Matt. "Mighty glad to know you. Was some real fine shooting, all right."

Buckman took the rawhider's beefy fingers into his own. "Proud to know you," he said. "Already told Hooker that I'm grateful to you all for saving my scalp from those Kiowas."

Fargo nodded, spat. "We most likely ain't seen the last of them yet."

"Probably ain't," Hooker agreed. "Them that we beat off will sure go rustle up the rest of their bunch and be back. Going to have to keep our eyes peeled for them." He turned to the third member of the hide hunters. "This here young fellow's named Rooster Drumm. Ain't been with me long, maybe a year now, but he's right good at doing what he's told. Shake hands with Matt Buckman, Rooster."

Drumm advanced and did as directed. "Howdy. Sure was some fine shooting you done. I don't figure I could hit the side of a barn the way that wagon was a-bouncing around, had it been me."

Rooster, as well as Fargo Smith, carried the stench of hides the same as Cud Hooker, Matt noted, but he suppressed the urge to grimace and managed a wry grin.

"Was my neck on the chopping block same as it was yours. Had to make my shots count. . . . Sure hate it about your friend Penmon getting his. I feel sort of responsible."

"Don't," Hooker said. "He knew what he was doing, same as the rest of us. Hell, we'll all be going under someday! Just a guess of how and when."

"Ain't no doubt of that," Fargo Smith said, and drew a pint bottle of whiskey from his hip pocket.

"Pen was a good old boy—one I was right pleased to ride with. I reckon we all ought to have us a drink for his sake."

Tipping the flat container to his lips Fargo had a swallow of the rotgut and then solemnly passed it on to Hooker. Cud took his drink, after which the bottle went to Matt, and finally to Rooster.

"Sure glad I ain't him," Drumm commented, smacking loudly. "Them redskins can really do a job on a man when they put their mind to it."

"They won't do nothing to him—he was dead," Cud said. "It's the live ones they dote on," he added, and unbuttoning his shirt and underwear displayed several knife scars on his chest and belly to Matt. "Can't nobody tell me nothing about Indians! I know them firsthand."

Pivoting, Hooker stalked off toward the creek, the muscles of his broad, thick shoulders stirring under the red fabric he was wearing.

Fargo pulled off his hat, mopped at the bald spot in the center of his head. "Don't say no more about Indians in front of him," he warned softly.

"Right," Rooster agreed hurriedly. "Don't want to get him started raving. Cud's hell to be around when he's all riled up."

Hooker had doubled back to the wagon, was lifting a wooden box from its bed. Carrying it over to a level place near the creek, he set it down.

"One of you get a fire going," he directed. "I'll dig into the grub box and see what I can turn up to eat. You much of a cook, Matt?"

"Some—"

"Can do some helping then. We've got salt pork

and beans, hardtack, coffee—you reckon you can brew us up some good, strong coffee?"

"Expect I can," Matt replied.

He'd find it hard to eat with the stink of the rawhiders all around him, but he was hungry, and he'd have no choice. On foot now, all his earthly belongings gone except what he was wearing, and miles from any settlement, there was nothing to do but accept the hide hunters' hospitality and make the best of it.

He still had his money, a hundred dollars more or less, safely stowed away in the belt around his middle, but he'd not mention it. He was far from comfortable with the rawhiders, especially Cud Hooker and Fargo Smith, and he had to hang on to his cash; somewhere along the way he'd get a chance to buy himself a horse and gear and he wanted to be certain he had the wherewithal to do so.

"Here's the pot," Hooker said, tossing a blackened granite vessel to Matt. "You'll have to do some pounding on the beans. Use a couple of rocks—we just ain't got no grinder," he continued, handing over a small muslin sack containing coffee.

Matt needed no instructions. He had prepared his own meals on the trail and in the line shacks hundreds of times, but he made no comment, simply set to work grinding the brown pellets between two stones and dumping the result into the pot. That done he crossed to the stream, filled the container with water, and returned to the fire Rooster had built.

Nearby Hooker was slicing salt pork into a skillet which already contained a quantity of cooked beans

—leftovers from a previous meal—while, squatted beside him, Fargo Smith hacked away at several of the hard, dry biscuits as he endeavored to cut them into more manageable chunks for heating.

The spider filled with meat, beans, and a quantity of water and set over the flames alongside the pot of coffee, Hooker drew back and found a seat on a nearby rock. He wore no guns, Matt saw, but carried two knives—a long-bladed one on his left hip, a curved, honed-to-razor's-edge skinning knife on his right.

"Reckon you're in a sort of a picklement, Matt," he said, clawing at the bit of litter and dried food trapped in his beard.

"Sure am," Buckman agreed.

"Where was you a-heading when them devils jumped you?"

"Dodge City—"

Fargo Smith, placing the chunks of hardtack on rocks about the fire, glanced up. "That's a mighty far piece from here."

"Fact is everywhere is mighty far from here," Rooster laughed. "We're right out in the big middle of nowhere."

"I been thinking," Hooker said, ignoring Drumm's humor, "us being short a man since old Pen went and got hisself turned into buzzard bait, maybe you'd like to throw in with us."

Matt brushed at the sweat on his jaws, shrugged. He could think of few things he'd like less, but again he had no option; he had no horse and gear, and besides he did feel a certain obligation to the rawhiders for saving him from the renegade Indians. And they did lose a member doing it.

"Ain't no big money in rawhiding," Hooker went on, "and what we get we split even Stephen. It'd be the same as when Penmon was here—a four-way cut."

"There much money in hides?" Matt asked, eyes on the pot of coffee, which was beginning to rumble as steam built up within it. "Always heard it was a mighty lean way of making a living."

"It ain't so bad," Hooker said, glancing at Fargo and Rooster. "We just sort of knock around picking up hides here and there where we can find them. Then when we get a load we haul them in to some town where there's a buyer—place like this here Dodge City you was going to, or maybe Denver or Abilene—and sell them off. Of course we make us a little side money, too," he added, again glancing at his two partners. There was a half smile on his heavy lips.

"Side money?" Matt wondered.

"Yeh, trading—buying and selling, and the like. Once come across a wagon some folks had gone off and left. We patched it up, sold it to a homesteader for twenty dollars."

Fargo laughed, thrust a handful of sticks into the fire. "Ain't exactly how it was, but I reckon it'll do for telling," he said.

Hooker bristled. His small, dark eyes narrowed. "You calling me a liar?"

Fargo waved him off. "Ain't said so, have I? Was just mentioning that it wasn't exactly like you said—but no matter. Don't count for nothing." Taking up a long-handled wooden spoon, he began to stir the beans and salt pork, which, despite the odor rising from the three men and the wagon, some twenty feet away, was filling the air with a good smell.

"Matt there could ride Pen's horse since he ain't got one," Rooster said. Drumm wore a pair of large Mexican spurs that touched the ground when he walked.

"Yeh, I reckon he could," Hooker said thoughtfully.

If matters went right the opportunity might arise where he could buy Penmon's horse and gear, Matt thought, either with some of the cash he was carrying or by taking the animal and the equipment as his share of money earned. He'd suggest it to Hooker when the time was right.

"Be real pleased to throw in with you," Matt said, going back to the rawhider's earlier suggestion. "I reckon I can hold up my end."

"Ain't no doubt in my mind," Cud said, "but I aim to change things a mite. You'll be driving the wagon, I'll be forking Pen's horse; leastwise that's how it'll be for a spell. . . . How about that java? It's boiling; ought to be ready."

Buckman, careful to show no disappointment in what was to be his job, drew his bandanna, and using it as a pad, lifted the pot off the fire. Laying back the lid he waited a bit for the dark contents to settle, and then taking a twig stirred down the froth.

"Stew's ready, too," Fargo announced. "Dig them plates and such out of the grub box, Rooster. I'm plenty hungry."

"It'd tasted better if you'd put some onions in it,"

Drumm grumbled, producing the tin plates, cups and spoons.

"Sure would've—if we'd had a onion or two," Hooker replied, taking up one of the plates and spooning a generous portion of the mixture into it. Reaching for a chunk of hardtack he shook his head. "Sure wisht we had us a woman to do the cooking."

"Did once," Fargo Smith said, taking over the wooden spoon and filling his dish, "but you just couldn't keep your hands off her."

"Hell, a woman's for something else besides doing cooking," Hooker said, pouring himself a cup of the coffee. "And it sure is a lot more fun than eating."

4

The town of Edom sprawled sun-bleached and wind-scoured along a narrow river many called the Upper Canadian in northeastern New Mexico Territory. The halting place for some pilgrims moving west for the promised land of California, it served not only as a supply and repair station but as a rest stop as well for those wearied from the empty, lonely miles that lay between there and the Missouri.

For Caleb Gannon reaching Edom was a tremendous relief. Mattie, his wife, had grown worse during those last two days on the trail, and he was anxious to get her to a doctor. Mattie's health had been the reason for their pulling up stakes and leaving their native Pennsylvania. She had broken down with consumption, their family physician back in Carlisle had advised them warning that if Mattie was to live she must be moved to a warm, dry climate. He had suggested either the territory of New Mexico or Arizona. Caleb chose the latter as the other sounded much too foreign for his Yankee taste.

After the Carlisle physician had delivered his verdict, Gannon had immediately put his hardware business up for sale. He found a buyer almost as promptly as it was a thriving, prosperous concern in a community that was expanding steadily. That all-important matter out of the way, he had then set about outfitting himself with a well-built wagon that he reinforced and made several other improvements on, and a strong team.

Once ready, Caleb had loaded up what family possessions they could not bear to leave and with their eighteen-year-old daughter, Holly, on the seat beside him, and Mattie made as comfortable as possible on a pallet in the bed of the vehicle, they had headed for Arizona.

Somewhat short of stature and a bit on the stout side, Gannon nevertheless carried an air of authority about him, owing no doubt to the success in business he had attained, and as a result he had found himself on the third day out of Independence in charge of a train of four wagons. It had all come about in a natural, expected way, and when the men of the other wagons had come to him with the request that he take over, he didn't object. Admittedly, there was little he knew about traveling across the vast reaches of a hostile land, but he figured if other men could do it, so also could he.

But Mattie's health had worsened, and now as he stood in front of the Edom doctor's combination office and home with Holly—pert in a dark-blue cotton dress, red-checked shirt, and white straw hat—at his side, he was giving serious thought to ending the pilgrimage west right then and there.

"I've got to do what's best for your mama," he said, "and I'm not sure just what that is."

Holly removed her hat, brushed at her dark, almost chestnut-brown hair. She had light blue eyes and firm, well-shaped lips, and was in all a very pretty young woman.

"What did the doctor say?"

"That your mama was weak—very bad. She's much worse than she was when we left home. I'm not sure we should even go on."

"You mean just not go any farther—but stay right here?"

Gannon, staring off toward the river where the rest of the wagon train had halted and made camp for the night, nodded. "Seems it might be best."

Holly shook her head. "Mama wouldn't want that. She'll never give up, and she wouldn't want us to."

Caleb's shoulders stirred. Sometimes it was wrong if you did and wrong if you didn't, and a man was left standing between a rock and a hard place unable to turn. His plans for the future, the three thousand dollars in cash that yet remained from the sale of his business and with which he intended to build a new life for his family and himself, meant nothing unless Mattie was a part of it—and it was beginning to look as if she might not be. But if they remained in Edom would her chances for survival be any better?

"You're right of course," Gannon said slowly. "Your mama was always a fighter. She'd want us to go on."

"Why couldn't we lay over here for today and tonight?" Holly suggested. "I know the doctor said we should get her to Arizona as soon as possible, but I think a little rest here would do her a world of good. We could go on in the morning, and when we come to another town lay over again for a day or so if she's doing poorly."

"I suppose that's best," Gannon said, for the first time in his life filled with indecision and uncertainty. "We'll get to Arizona when we can. If it takes a few more weeks, or even months, then that's how it will be. All that matters is that we make it."

"True," Caleb murmured, his gaze again on the wagons gathered along the Canadian. A number of the children were playing in the shallows of the stream, their laughter and shouts a bright, carefree sound riding the warm air. "Expect we'll just have to do the best we can, and if the good Lord's willing, we'll get to Wickenburg."

"Don't worry, Papa, we will," Holly said reassuringly. "Do you want me to go tell Mama?"

Caleb gave that a few moments' thought and nodded. "Probably would be better for you to. Just say we're staying over here in Edom to rest the team, and do some repairing on the wagon. I don't want her to realize she is worse."

"All right, I'll be careful what I say. Where will you be?"

Gannon pointed at their wagon, halted in the shade of a large hackberry tree at the side of the physician's home. They had brought Mattie out after the man had completed his examination, and returned her to the pallet bed of the canvas-arched vehicle.

"I'll drive on back to the others. They'll need to be told to go on."

"Looks like they're about ready to start now,"

Holly said, studying the party along the river. "I think they'll wait if you ask them to."

"It would probably be a good idea. We're getting into that part of the country where the Indians are said to be hostile—or at least some of them. There's safety in us traveling together; but I'll leave it up to them," Gannon said, and with Holly at his side started toward the wagon. "As far as we're concerned we can catch up in a day or two. The teams they're driving won't travel very fast."

"Yes, I know—"

"I can make good use of a day off the trail," Caleb continued. "There's some harness that needs mending, and I ought to go over the wagon, see if everything is holding up like it should."

"Don't forget to fill the water barrels—"

"I won't. And you best see to the larder in case we're getting low on anything. Edom is the last town of any size we'll come to for a while, so I was told, so we had better stock up here."

"I already have a list, Papa," Holly said, pausing at the corner of the physician's yard. "I'll take care of it now and talk to Mama later."

Caleb nodded and continued on to the wagon. The girl watched him put a foot on the hub of the near front wheel, grasp the iron rail of the seat, and pull himself up into the vehicle. Taking up the lines he half turned, said something to her mother, and then, with a slap of the reins on the horses' broad backs, started them moving off toward the river.

They were fine animals, Holly thought, remembering how her father had scouted around Carlisle and the surrounding area for the best horses he could find that could stand the long journey to Arizona. Dun-colored geldings would be the answer, he'd learned from men who had made several trips West. They withstood the hot sun best and were less susceptible to harness gall.

Finding a pair of the gray-brown horses had not been easy, but finally in Harrisburg, a town a few miles east of Carlisle, he located a team and purchased them immediately. He had to pay far too much for them, Caleb had told her, but he wanted the best—for it would take the best in horseflesh to get them to Arizona.

Holly came about and started leisurely toward Edom's only general store. She had hated giving up her life in Carlisle and leaving behind all her friends, just as her mother and father had. But there was nothing else to be done. Anyway, she'd be able to start a new life in Arizona—in Wickenburg. It would be fun making new friends.

But Wickenburg was far away, she thought with a sigh as she climbed the three steps fronting the general store and started across its landing cluttered with merchandise—washtubs, water buckets, horse collars, and such. She could only pray that her mother could stand the rigors of the journey and that they would once again have a home.

5

"Me and Fargo are going out and do a little scouting around," Cud Hooker said, reaching into the wagon and bringing forth a mariner's brass telescope. "Sure ain't had no luck lately."

Fargo Smith was tightening the cinch of the saddle on the thick-bodied black horse he rode. "For a fact. About time we turned up something," he said, sourly.

They had finished with the evening meal, but it was still early—three hours at least until darkness.

"You boys just set tight," Hooker continued, directing his attention to Matt and Rooster Drumm. "If it happens I need the wagon I'll send Fargo to fetch you. Meantime you can be fixing up camp for the night."

Rooster swore angrily, and jerking off his hat slapped it against his leg in disgust. "Damn it, Cud, I sure didn't sign on with this outfit to be no swamper! I—"

"Won't hurt you none," Hooker cut in mildly as he swung up onto Penmon's horse. Shifting about in the saddle for several moments as he sought comfort, the rawhider swore. "Got to let out these stirrups. Too dang short for me." He paused, looked hopefully at Matt and then Rooster as if expecting one of them to step up and do the job for him. Neither made any move. Shrugging, Hooker wheeled his horse about and started out of the clearing.

"Reckon I can put up with it for a while," he said, and gestured to Fargo Smith. "Come on, let's go," and as the heavyset man swung his horse in beside him, added: "It's getting late."

Buckman watched the pair ride out and turned to the fire. Moving to where he was upwind of Rooster, he poured himself a cup of coffee and settled on his heels. The frying pan that the stew had been cooked in, plates, cups, and other items used for the meal were yet in need of cleaning. Evidently the chore fell to him and Rooster.

"I hear Hooker say you'd been with him for about a year?"

Drumm, removing his spurs, laid them on a nearby rock. Dropping to a hunch, he took up the coffeepot and filled his cup. The brew was strong and black, had been simmering over the fire for some time.

"Just about, and I'm thinking it's long enough," Rooster replied.

"Why don't you move on? All you've got to do is climb onto your horse and ride out."

"Yeh, I know that, only times when I get the notion I get to thinking about the money I get when the sharing comes, and the good fun we have when we go to one of them big towns. Couldn't do that if I was punching cows for some rancher—or make as much money, either."

"Your share of the cash usually pretty good?"

Matt asked, still unable to see how there could be much profit in rawhiding for four partners.

"Damn right," Rooster said with a laugh. "It ain't regular wages like a fellow working on a ranch, but when we sell off the split's real good. But for me it's mostly going into some big town, like I said, and having myself a time doing a lot of drinking and gambling and dancing, and having women—just plain old hell-raising you might call it. Sure is worth working for. You ever done much of that?"

Matt shrugged, downed the last of his coffee, and set the cup aside. "Yeh, I've been to a few of those places—"

"I'm betting you ain't never done nothing like me and Cud and the others have—and I reckon, come brimstone or black water, I'll keep right on doing it. Can't think of no better way of making a living."

"Sounded like you'd about got a bellyful a bit ago when you were talking to Cud."

"Oh, hell, he sort of gets under a man's hide now and then. You just have to learn how to handle him —kind of show your teeth once in a while so's he won't run over you, but still stay real friendly like."

"He's a big sucker—"

"Sure is, and strong as a mule. I've seen him skin a dry carcass, one that's stiff and hard as nails, in less than a hour—a fresh kill in half that."

"What's he got against Indians? Seems to hate them mighty bad."

Rooster frowned, sloshed the remainder of his coffee about in the cup. "Well, I ain't for certain I ought to be telling things like that, but I reckon it'll be all right seeing as how you're going to be one of us—"

Matt shook his head. "Don't crawl out on a limb for me. I was just wondering about it."

Drumm's shoulders stirred indifferently. "Was a few years back—long before me or even Fargo teamed up with him. Happened somewhere over in the Indian Territory country. Seems he come across a young Indian gal taking herself a swim in a river. Cud's got a powerful yen for women. Just can't leave them alone.

"Anyways, he sneaks up on the gal, drags her off into the brush and was having himself a time with her when some braves from her tribe come along. They took Cud back to their village, tied him to a post, and worked him over good with knives and burning sticks for a couple of days and nights. You seen his front side—his belly and chest. They ain't near as bad as his back. Hell, there's two places big as a man's hand on his ass where they held a red-hot lance point or axhead.

"He finally got hisself loose one night when everybody was sleeping, grabbed a horse, and got away. So he's had it in for Indians ever since. I've seen him take his rifle and shoot down a redskin that wasn't doing nothing but riding by—one of the friendlies, not a hostile."

"Indians don't like white men fooling with their women any more than white men like Indians fooling with theirs," Matt commented. "What was that about a woman cook that he and Fargo were talking about?"

"Oh, ain't much to that. We sort of took over a

couple and their wagon a year or so ago. The man, well, he up and died, and the woman, being caught out here all by herself, kind of hired on to be our cook.

"Was a good one, too, but Cud, being the way he is when it comes to a woman, couldn't keep his hands off her. Had her up in the back of the wagon most of the time, and she just sort of quit trying to do her cooking chores."

"What happened to her?"

Rooster finished off his coffee and dangled the empty cup from a forefinger as he stared into the ashes of the fire. "One day she grabbed a hold of Hooker's rifle and blew her brains out. Just couldn't take no more of him, I expect. Shame, too, because we was eating real good."

"How long ago was that?"

"Month or so, maybe a bit less. You been working on some ranch around here?"

Matt nodded. "Place to the south and west of here. Quit a while back. Was on my way to catch me a train ride to Chicago, see the sights."

"Chicago—ain't never been there."

"Me neither, but I've heard some talk about it. They say it's a right interesting place to go to."

"You still aiming to?"

Matt gave that thought. He was still searching for a way to leave the rawhiders and continue on to Dodge City, but without a horse there was no way of doing so. He considered, briefly, taking Rooster into his confidence, and discussing the possibility of buying—or borrowing—Penmon's mount, but put the idea aside. He didn't know Drumm well enough yet and was unsure how the man would take it. Best to wait until they were better acquainted and then attempt to persuade Rooster to help him get a horse.

"Yeh, one of these days. Man goes there, though, he wants to have plenty in his poke."

Rooster tossed his empty cup into the frying pan, the clatter frightening off a pair of scrub jays probing about the wagon.

"Hearing you talk about it kind of makes me want to go there myself," Drumm said. "You reckon we could team up some day—maybe after Cud sells off what we got, and we get our split—and go there together?"

Hope stirred anew within Matt Buckman. There just might be a chance of getting away from the rawhiders sooner than he expected.

"Sure, why not? Maybe when Hooker sells off the load of hides we've got now."

"Maybe so," Rooster said, rising, "but we ain't got much to sell yet. . . . Expect we'd best see to the team. Cud's a great one for fine horses but he don't never think anything about taking care of them. You want to give me a hand?"

"Sure," Matt replied, coming to his feet and following Drumm to the wagon. "You ever come across any horses running loose, like one that maybe belonged to some Indian or maybe a pilgrim that got himself killed, when you're out looking for hides?"

"Oh, sure," Rooster said. "If they ain't worth much we just shoot them and skin them out, but if they're pretty fair looking stock, and there ain't no brand on them, we sell them off to somebody." He paused, glanced at Matt. "Why, you wanting a horse?"

"Indians got mine back there, along with all my gear. Kind of like to start fixing myself up with a new outfit."

"Won't need one. Cud ain't going to do no riding on that horse of Penmon's long. He'll be ready to climb back onto the seat of that wagon mighty soon because he just ain't used to forking a horse."

Matt, enduring the terrible odor coming from the interior of the wagon, assisted Rooster in freeing the horses from the vehicle—slipping the bridles but leaving the rest of the harness in place—and leading them down to the stream for watering.

"Can picket them there on that patch of grass," Drumm said, pointing to a small square of green on the opposite side of the creek. "Reckon I'd best get my horse and tie him up over there, too. . . . That stink bothering you?"

Matt, unaware that Rooster had been watching him closely, grinned. "Sure is fierce—and I'm going to be setting up there in that wagon driving, come tomorrow."

"Bothered me plenty at first, too," Drumm said, "but you'll get used to it."

Buckman smiled again. "Ain't so sure of that," he said, and turned back to the camp. "I'll rustle up these pots and dishes, give them a cleaning."

"Yeh, seems we've got that damned chore pushed off on us, too. Was I to have my way they'd do their eating off dirty dishes, else clean them themselves."

Rooster paused, looked off onto the plain beyond Matt. "Here they come."

Buckman raised his eyes to the flat, now all amber and gray-green in the late afternoon light. Riding at an easy lope, Cud Hooker and Fargo Smith were just coming into view.

"Sure hope they got something spotted," Rooster said. "Ain't hardly turned a hand in weeks."

6

Matt Buckman, accustomed to rising early, found himself the only one up and about at daybreak that next morning. Cud, Rooster, and Fargo Smith continued to snore in their blanket rolls as Matt, at a loss to comprehend this departure from the ranch life routine he had followed for years, looked around for something to pass the time until the others awoke and were on their feet.

He crossed to where the horses had been picketed, thinking as he did that sleeping in was no doubt part of the good life Rooster had spoken of, and had brief wonder if he could ever get used to it. He decided quickly that it didn't matter; he wouldn't be around that long—actually no longer than it took to find a way out.

The horses were dozing also. They had apparently fared well on the grass where they had spent the night. Coming back around, Matt retraced his steps to camp. The rawhiders were still asleep, and moving quietly Buckman built a fire and got a pot of coffee under way. He was hunched, back to one of the numerous cottonwood trees that grew along the creek, enjoying a cup of the steaming brew, when Fargo Smith rolled out of his blanket and joined him.

"What the hell got you up so damned early?" the older man demanded irritably as he filled his cup from the pot.

"Habit, I reckon," Matt replied.

"Well, you best get out of it," Fargo said, squatting by the fire. The chill was noticeable at that early hour in the high plains country.

"What's going on?" Cud Hooker asked, sitting up and looking about. "Them Kiowas back?"

"No, just this here new partner of our'n," Fargo said. "Likes to get up with the chickens. Ain't got it in his head yet that he ain't on no regular job—and that we come and go when we please, eat when we like, and sleep all day if we're of the notion."

"Now, that's how it is, Buckman," Hooker said. "You best remember it."

A half smile cracked Matt's lips. The rawhiders were making a mighty big mountain out of a pretty small molehill, it seemed to him. But he'd keep his mouth shut and let it pass. Important thing was to get along with the rawhiders until he got the chance to pull out.

Hooker, nursing a bottle of whiskey, eyes heavy from sleep, joined Fargo at the fire. Moments later Rooster Drumm roused and took a place beside them, and for a time all three sat hunched about the low flames, each palming a cup of Buckman's steaming brew in their two hands.

"Sure got to say this," Fargo commented, nodding to Matt, "you sure make a real fine cup of java."

Rooster mumbled something, apparently seconding the approval. Hooker yawned, looked up.

"You good at cooking vittles, too?"

Matt shrugged. His chances for getting away from the rawhiders and the sickening stench that went with them might be improved if he took on the chore of cooking. There would be grub to buy, which meant going to a general store somewhere; the opportunity he looked for would then be at hand.

"Fed myself plenty of times, and I'm still living—"

"Well, you start fixing us something right now while me and Fargo and Rooster get ready to pull out."

"You got something spotted?" Drumm asked eagerly.

"Yep, me and Fargo sighted a wagon making camp up the trail a ways just before we headed back to here yesterday. I figure we can meet them along that grove east of here around the middle of the morning."

"A rich-looking outfit?"

"Maybe. Was kind of hard to tell, but I reckon it'll be worth while."

"Leastwise it will be for Cud, because there's a woman along," Fargo said caustically, setting his cup down and getting to his feet.

Hooker eyed his partner silently for a few moments, rid himself of his cup, and also rose. Tension abruptly filled the cool, motionless air, and the promise of violence suddenly hung like powder smoke over the camp.

Rooster hastily drew himself upright and stepped

in front of Hooker. A concerned frown knotted his brow.

"Cud, you see any sign of them renegade Indians that had Matt cornered yesterday when you were out looking around? Sure as soon not run into them again."

Hooker made no reply for a long minute, and then his taut shoulders relaxed. "Nope, didn't," he said, and shifted his glance to Matt, digging into the grub box in search of food for the meal. "Give Buckman there a hand if he's needing it. Won't hurt none if you help him right along. Can do the dishwashing—"

"The hell with that!" Drumm shouted angrily. "I'm for every man washing his own—just like we've been doing."

Hooker laughed, adjusted the leather sheaths of the knives he wore to the back of his hips. "Was maybe funning you about that—but you help him just the same."

Rooster wagged his head. "I know you and your funning. Usually works out that you ain't."

Hooker, moving off toward the horses, said nothing. Matt, pondering the earlier conversation between the three men concerning the pilgrim sighted up the trail, was realizing now that some of his suspicions concerning the rawhiders were probably true—that hide-hunting was just a cover-up for robbery. If such proved to be a fact he'd find himself in a bad spot; he would be implicated in their crimes and considered just as guilty as they even though he did not actually take a hand in the holdups.

But there was nothing he could do for the time

being but string along with them, he decided, digging out several potatoes, the side of salt pork, and more hardtack as the basis for the meal. Setting to work with what was available, he got the breakfast under way. Nearby Rooster did his part by building up the fire and adding more water to the coffeepot.

When the meal was over Hooker wiped greasy hands on his thighs and nodded approvingly. "Weren't too bad figuring what you had to work with."

"That's the problem," Buckman said, his hopes rising. "We're about out of everything. When will we come to a town where I can stock up?"

Hooker shook his head. "Ain't no town within seventy-five, maybe a hundred miles of here."

Matt hid his disappointment for a second time. "Well, we better get some grub somewhere—"

"Don't go fretting over it," Hooker said, finishing off his second cup of coffee. "We'll be stocking up real soon." Features hardening, he looked at Fargo. "You ready?"

Smith nodded, set his plate on the ground, and got to his feet. Rooster Drumm followed suit quickly.

"Reckon we both are, Cud," Rooster replied.

Hooker turned again to Buckman. "Soon as you're done cleaning up here, load up the wagon and head out northeast, toward that high peak you can see off there a ways. We'll be scouting on ahead."

Matt signified his understanding, watched the men mount and ride out. When they were gone he collected the cooking and other utensils and washed

them in the stream, all the while simmering with
anger at the situation he found himself in; he could
do nothing but go along with the rawhiders; like a
man sitting in on a high-stakes poker game, he
could do nothing but play the cards dealt him.

Returning the pots and pans to the chuck box, he
loaded it into the foul-smelling wagon, hitched up
the team, and moved out, his eyes on the distant
peak that was to serve as his marker.

There was no sign of the rawhiders, and Matt
reckoned they had headed into the trees on the far
side of the plain that spread out, fresh and gray-
green-looking in the early morning sunlight, before
him. No longer blinded by the belief that Hooker
and his partners depended upon hides for their
source of income but instead preyed upon travelers
passing along the trail, he was dreading what lay
ahead, and if there had been the smallest possibility
that he could have fled with the wagon he would
have done so. But with the three men on horseback
he knew he'd not get far in the heavy wagon before
they overtook and cut him down.

He caught sight of the men a time later. They
appeared briefly along the edge of a grove and then
disappeared again into its shadowy depths. Buckman, the location of the rawhiders now established
in his mind, continued on, allowing the horses to
choose their own pace as they crossed the broad
flat.

The day was bright and clear and already turning
hot. Here and there horned larks sprang up into the
air when startled by the passing of the team, and
several times Matt saw rabbits scurrying off into the

short weeds. Quail were plentiful, coveys often bursting into flight at the approach of the wagon. All in all it was a fine day marred only by what he feared he would find awaiting him when he rejoined the rawhiders.

An hour or so later, as he drew near a bend in the grove, the sound of gunshots reached Matt. Drawing the team to a halt, he stood up for a better look at the country ahead of him. He was unsure where the shots had come from—and of what they might mean. As to the former it seemed logical for the shooting to have erupted somewhere in the trees around the bend, but the cause was not so apparent; Hooker and the others could have encountered Turkey Feather and a party of his braves, or they could have come up against a pilgrim who resisted being robbed.

At any rate he had no choice but to go on, join Cud Hooker and his partners. If it was the renegade Kiowas, they would need his help; and if it was a holdup in progress, well, he had no choice but to become a part of that, too. At that moment Matt saw Rooster Drumm in the distance ride out from the fringe of trees and urgently signal him to come. Settling back onto the seat Buckman popped the horses with the lines and sent them trotting toward the rawhider.

7

Reaching the point where he had seen Rooster Drumm, Matt veered the team off the rutted road and pointed for a clearing in the trees where he could see Rooster, now off his horse, waiting for him.

Nearby was a small canvas-topped wagon. A man lay dead near its left front wheel, and beyond it a short distance were two horses, also dead. Fargo Smith was rummaging about under the canvas arch of the vehicle, and as Buckman drew to a halt Cud Hooker emerged from a stand of brush at the edge of the clearing. Sickened, angry, he brought his team to a halt.

"What the hell—" he began, and then broke off as he caught a glimpse of another body showing whitely in the thicket where Hooker had been. Matt had been compelled to accept the fact of holdups where the rawhiders were concerned, but murder was something else.

"You finding anything worth taking?" he heard Cud call to Fargo Smith as he stopped at the tailgate of the wagon. Hooker's eyes were bright, his heavy features flushed, and there was a streak of blood in his beard where he had apparently been scratched.

"Ain't much," Fargo replied. Evidently the hostil-

ity that had sprung up between the two men had
dissipated, as they now seemed to be on good
terms.

Buckman wrapped the lines about the whipstock
and dropped to the ground. Rooster grinned at
him.

"Sure took your time. Was about to start out after
you when I seen you coming."

"Didn't figure there was any big hurry till I heard
the shooting. Thought maybe those Kiowas had
jumped you."

"Naw, was just us taking care of things here,"
Drumm said, and moved off toward the pilgrims'
wagon, halted beside it, and began to paw through
the odds and ends of clothing that Fargo had tossed
out as he searched for items of value. At that moment Smith glanced up. He beckoned to Matt.

"Come on over here and get this box of grub—"

Buckman, eyes on the body in the thicket—that of
a woman, he now saw—shook off his shock and
disgust and crossing slowly to the pilgrims' vehicle
picked up the wooden box of foodstuff and carried
it to the rawhiders' wagon.

"What the hell's the matter with him?" Matt
heard Hooker ask. "He figure he's too good to do
some helping out?"

"No, I reckon he's just a mite surprised," Rooster
answered. "Don't think he was looking to find
something like this."

"Well, he better get used to it," Hooker said in a
loud voice. "He joined up with us—and he surer'n
hell's going to stay joined."

"Don't get all riled up, Cud," Rooster said. "He'll

come around all right. We've got to give him the chance to learn how we—"

"He best get straight with us right soon—I ain't going to have nobody hanging around that's not one of us," Hooker said, his implication clear. "You turn up any cash money?" he added, putting his attention on Fargo.

"Fifty, sixty dollars, thereabouts. Was in the old man's pockets. You find anything on the woman?"

"Couple of rings. Won't be worth much," Cud replied with an indifferent shrug of his shoulders. "What's in that trunk?"

"Bunch of old pictures and papers. They sure didn't have much—just traveling, living hand-to-mouth, hoping they'd make to wherever they was heading."

Matt, standing at the side of the team, listened in angry silence to the conversation. Seeing a dead man was no new experience to him, nor was the stripped body of a murdered woman; he had been called upon to help clean up a massacre several times in his life—but this was different: this was the cold-blooded murder of two human beings.

"You have to kill them?" he demanded, finding his voice.

Fargo, still inside the wagon, paused, looked up, and faced Buckman. Hooker moved out from behind the vehicle while Rooster Drumm ceased his pawing about in the articles strewn about on the ground.

"Now just what the hell did you figure we'd do? Let them keep on going till they come to some town where they could tell the law all about us?" Cud's voice was thick with sarcasm.

"Was told by you there wasn't a town within seventy-five or a hundred miles of here. We would have had plenty of time to get clean out of this part of the country."

"Expect we would, but I kind of like it along here. It's real quiet and lonesome," Hooker said quietly, moving a few steps closer to Matt. Powerful shoulders thrown forward, muscular arms hanging at his sides, huge fists clenched into rock-hard clubs, he stared at Buckman through half-shut eyes. "I'm wondering a mite about you, mister."

"He's all right—told you that already, Cud," Rooster said hurriedly. "You got to give him a chance to learn about us, and—"

Matt waved Drumm to silence. "I can do my own talking," he said, watching Hooker closely.

The rawhider had halted, was continuing to study him with his cold, dark eyes. He'd made a bad mistake, Matt realized, one that could cost him his life if he wasn't careful. Hooker as well as Fargo Smith was now suspicious, and most likely they were having doubts as to his reliability. And he could expect Rooster Drumm, who was doing his best to smooth matters over for him, would soon assume the same attitude.

"Still say you didn't have to kill them," Matt said, his tone relenting. "With them heading on west we could've been on Colorado by the time they got to where they could talk to somebody."

"Reckon we could've," Hooker said, relaxing slightly, "but that ain't how I want it."

Buckman shrugged. "You're the head man, which gives you the say-so. But murder is something mighty bad. It can keep the law dogging a man's heels for years."

"Not the way we fix it," Hooker said, "and we've been going along for quite a spell now without nobody bothering us."

"That's the truth," Fargo said. He had climbed up onto the seat of the wagon and was listening idly to what was being said. "Cud and me've got this here down to a system, and it's done real good for us."

"Every time you pull a holdup do you shoot the folks that're in the wagon?"

"Reckon that all depends, but mostly it's safer," Rooster said. "We don't bother much with outfits like this," he continued. "Ain't worth the trouble, 'cepting for grub and the like."

"We keep our eyes peeled for the real fine rigs," Fargo said. "They'll be the ones carrying plenty of cash, and a trunk full of silverware—stuff we can sell."

"Law ain't caught up with us yet!" Rooster pointed out proudly.

Matt took advantage of the statement to improve his precarious position with the rawhiders. "Well, I sure hope it don't! I ain't anxious to have a rope around my neck!"

Hooker, apparently reassured by Buckman's attitude and back to his usual self again, nodded. "You just do what you're told and nothing like that'll ever happen to you. The law ain't got no idea about us other'n that we're rawhiders, and we're all real careful to keep it that way. Now, you get busy with

Rooster. He knows what to keep and what ain't worth nothing. I've got to skin out them two nags."

Matt sighed inwardly, relieved that the tight moments he'd let himself in for had passed. He couldn't be absolutely certain that he had convinced Hooker and the others of his loyalty, but he had leveled things off for the time being at least.

However, the incident pointed up all the more a need to get away from the hide-hunting outlaws before he became involved so deeply in their murderous activities that he'd never be able to clear his name. He had to find a way, somehow.

Crossing to where Rooster was moving about in the clothing and other articles tossed from the wagon by Fargo Smith, he began to follow Drumm's example, picking up and examining each piece carefully.

"There ain't nothing here but old worn-out duds, and they won't bring a copper," Rooster said disgustedly. "We sure did pick us a skinny goose this time. I can't find nothing worth keeping."

Hooker, busy with his knives at one of the horses, glanced up but did not stop the quick, sure motions of the particular blade he was using at the moment.

"Sure too bad that all these pilgrims ain't rich folks," he said acidly. "We could make us a big pile of money quick and easy then. . . . If you're done messing with that stuff throw it over close to the wagon so's we can set it all afire."

"Can start anytime," Fargo said, coming down from his perch on the seat. "Ain't nothing in here."

"Then get over here and give me a hand," Hooker said. "Ain't no use us hanging around here any longer than needful. There just might be some better pickings up the trail a piece, and we sure want to be ready if there is."

"I'm sure hoping we'll find us a better one than this'n," Rooster commented.

"Won't be hard to do," Hooker said. "This here hayshaker was just something we took on because we were needing grub."

Fargo laughed, toyed with the gold watch chain looping across his belly. "Didn't notice you missing out none with that woman—"

Hooker paused, glanced up, and grinned. "I don't never miss out on a woman," he said, and resumed his work with the skinning knife. Again he hesitated, put his attention on Drumm. "Rooster, you and Buckman see to burying the woman and her man. Do like always—stick a couple of arrows in them, and scatter a few more around."

Rooster nodded and, beckoning to Matt, circled to the rear of the rawhiders' wagon. Reaching in under the stiff, malodorous hides, he obtained a handful of arrows. Passing them to Matt, he took the spade wedged under a brace on the side of the wagon bed, and moved off in the direction of the thicket where the woman's body lay. Midway he paused and faced Buckman.

"You sure ought to watch what you're saying to Cud. He's a real mean one when he gets riled—as soon blow your head off as not. . . . I'll go on, start digging. You get the old man's body and drag it over here. Can bury him and his woman together."

Matt, about to make a reply concerning Hooker,

thought better of it and turned back to the wagon. Halting beside the dead pilgrim, a middle-aged man in worn homesteader's clothing, he grasped the man by the wrists and started to drag him the short distance to the brush. On second thought he halted, picked up a wool blanket thrown from the wagon by Fargo, and hanging it over a shoulder, again began to move the unfortunate pilgrim.

"What's that for?" Fargo asked, pointing at the woolen cover.

"Cover the bodies," Buckman replied without stopping. "I figure they're entitled to a decent burial."

"Hell, they won't know nothing about it either way," Fargo said, and resumed the chore of assisting Hooker in skinning the horses.

Rooster had hollowed out a shallow trench and laid the battered body of the woman in it when Matt reached there. Saying nothing, the rawhider dragged the man's body into the narrow grave and placed it alongside that of the woman. Then, taking one of the arrows, he plunged it into the homesteader's chest and stepped back.

"I reckon that's that," he said, and pointing to the spade added: "I dug the hole for them, you can cover them over."

Grim, jaw set, Matt spread the blanket over the corpses and began to cover them with the loose soil. When he had finished with the task, he came about. Rooster had returned to the pilgrims' wagon and was tossing the items that had been thrown from the weathered old vehicle into a pile underneath it. Farther over Fargo Smith was laying the pliant, bloody hide of one of the horses on the stack inside the rawhiders' wagon, while Hooker was just finishing the chore of skinning the other.

"They a-resting in peace?" Fargo asked in a jocular tone as Buckman jammed the spade back into its holder.

"They're buried, if that's what you're getting at," Matt replied coldly.

In the next moment Cud Hooker, sweating profusely, blood on his hands and arms, and dragging the hide of the second horse behind him, drew up at the vehicle's tailgate. Picking up the limp skin, he tossed it into the wagon for Fargo to spread out over the others.

"Getting close to eating time," Hooker said, mopping his brow with a forearm. "We about ready to move out?"

"Sure are," Rooster said. "Just need setting the fire and scattering some of these here arrows about."

"Well, get at it," Cud snapped, and jerked his head at Matt. "I'll drive the wagon, you bring my horse. We'll head back to the creek."

Fargo, dropping from the bed of the vehicle, crossed to where he had tied his mount. "Ain't no need doubling clear back there. If we angle sort of west from here we'll come to it. Be shorter."

"Suits me," Hooker said, climbing up to the seat. Settling himself, he looked at Rooster. "Don't go fooling around here too long," he added, and clucked the team into motion.

Buckman, relieved that he wouldn't be required to drive the hide wagon, took up the reins of his and

Rooster Drumm's horses and led them aside. Hooker, preceded by Fargo Smith, moved out of the small clearing and struck directly off across the flat. Rooster, after first setting fire to the mound of clothing, papers, pieces of furniture, and other odds and ends under and around the pilgrims' vehicle, hurriedly began to scatter a half dozen or so of the flint- and metal-headed arrows about. That done he dropped back to Matt's side.

"I reckon that's it," he said, glancing at the spiral of dark smoke twisting up into the sky. "Things sure went off without a hitch—couldn't have been no better unless them folks had had a poke full of cash and a trunk of silverware."

The fire was now burning fiercely, the flames having licked their way up the side of the vehicle and caught the canvas top. Rooster swung up into his saddle.

"You ready to ride? We best get away from here fast. Somebody's liable to see that smoke."

Matt nodded as he mounted his horse. He was wishing he could climb aboard and keep going until he reached a town where he could talk to a lawman, tell him about the outlaw rawhiders, and rid himself of his forced association with them. But he knew there was no chance of that. Rooster Drumm, despite his friendliness, would be loyal to Hooker and their way of life and would not hesitate to kill him, Matt knew, if he attempted to desert.

8

"Do you think the layover did Mama any good?" Holly asked, looking back over her shoulder at the slowly fading blur on the horizon that was Edom.

"Hard to say," Caleb Gannon replied noncommittally, slapping the horses with the slack in the lines.

They had gotten an early start that morning, but Gannon knew it would be necessary to push the dun team hard to overtake the three other wagons of the train that had gone on ahead the day before.

"Maybe the new medicine the doctor gave her will help. It does seem to make her sleep more," the girl continued as she resumed her position. Caleb was in a dispirited mood and she had been trying to cheer him ever since they left the settlement.

"I doubt if anything will help much till we get to Arizona—and Arizona is a long ways off."

"I know, but we'll get there in time," Holly said now, looking back into the wagon where her mother lay quietly, eyes closed, on the pallet. "And she'll get well once we're there, Papa."

Gannon shook his head, leaned forward, and rested his elbows on his knees. "The cure won't be quick," he said, taking up the slack that had developed in the lines. "It'll take a long time—years, so the doctor said."

"I know—rest and sunshine, that will be the best medicine. She'll be all right. I know she'll get well."

Gannon made no comment as he continued to urge the horses on. Studying him for several moments, Holly said: "Are you worried about what that man back in Edom said about the Indians?"

"Some. It would be foolish not to."

"But I understood that things were all right between the white people and them, that there was a peace."

"There is, and it's held for several years, but the trouble we're having is with renegade braves. There are outlaws among the Indians same as there are among us. . . . I'll feel a lot better when we catch up to the rest of the train."

"When will that be?"

Gannon shrugged. "Maybe by day after tomorrow. They're traveling slow."

Holly wished they could reach Wickenburg in that short a time, but the territory was still far in the distance. She wondered what it would be like there. Surely it would be more civilized than some of the towns they had passed through, being one of Arizona's principal settlements.

She wished she could look forward to making a life of her own once they were there—become a schoolteacher or maybe open a ladies' clothing store. Holly had always had visions of striking out on her own but circumstances had dictated otherwise.

She didn't regret the role in life that had been

thrust upon her—that of being a nurse for her mother and a housekeeper for her father—but there were times when she resented the unfairness of it. Holly was in her midteens when her mother had fallen ill with the lung disease that made of her an invalid and put her to bed, where she had neither improved nor grown worse until a bit more than a year ago. At that time the consumption had abruptly become critical and the physician attending her had warned that unless the change in climate he recommended was made, Mattie would have but a short time to live.

It had been hard to accept the doctor's ultimatum but Holly had done so dutifully and without protest, for the life of her mother came first and above all else. Still it was difficult to give up all her dreams, all her friends, ones with whom she had grown up, attended school, and made plans for the future. It had meant the abandonment of her hopes of going to the university there in Carlisle and earning for herself a degree and then becoming a teacher or a librarian, or of perhaps marrying and having a family of her own.

Holly had never had any serious boyfriends. The brief, passing puppy-love affairs that all girls and boys experience in grammar and high school were the extent of such; there was neither time nor opportunity for the deeper relationships once she reached young womanhood, as her obligations at home claimed her completely.

Maybe that would all change once they were settled in Wickenburg and her mother began to mend. Maybe she'd meet a man and fall in love with him.

Arizona could mean a new beginning for her, too, Holly thought dreamily as the wagon rolled steadily across a near level flat. But she really should have an understanding with her father.

Once her mother's recovery was evident, she'd make him aware that she had a life of her own to live. She would insist that he hire a woman to assume the household chores along with a nurse to care for her mother's needs. Her father had plenty of money to do that; he'd come away with several thousand dollars after the sale of the hardware store, so paying for a nurse and a housekeeper would not work a financial hardship on him.

He intended to get into a business of some kind in Wickenburg—probably hardware again, according to what her mother had said. The settlement was a quite active mining center, and there was much demand for the kind of articles that he would be stocking in his store. He should do well, just as he had back in Carlisle, but then her father, Holly thought with pride, was the sort of man who would do well anywhere.

Maybe she should think about going into business. Perhaps if she could come up with a sound idea she could persuade him to finance her—with a loan, of course; she didn't expect him to just give her the money.

A herd of tan-and-white antelope burst suddenly from the low hills off to their left and raced off ahead of the horses. In the brilliant sunlight they looked to be sheathed with gold.

"Aren't they beautiful, Papa?" Holly asked, rousing from her reverie.

Caleb Gannon grunted his agreement. "Don't know if they're fit to eat or not," he said, Yankee practicality coming to the fore. "We could use some fresh meat."

But if Gannon had any idea of using the rifle lying at his feet he was too slow to do so as the antelope were quickly lost in the distance and well out of range.

"Maybe we'll see some deer," Holly suggested.

Gannon shook his head, leaned back on the seat. "Doubt it. Not much of anything in this godforsaken country but wolves and coyotes and other useless varmints. Not like back home. A man could take his gun, travel a mile or so, and find plenty of game."

"There were those antelope," the girl pointed out. "Bound to be deer and other animals around—"

"Ought to be, but I expect the Indians have killed them off."

The thought of Indians had slipped Holly's mind. A frown clouded her features. "Do you think we'll have any trouble with them?"

"It's anybody's guess—and a matter of luck, I suppose," Gannon replied. "There were those rumors of a war party that we heard back in Edom. Never actually talked to anybody who had been bothered, however."

"But it is possible, isn't it?"

"Of course—renegades that've broken off from their tribes, and gone out on their own. Nothing unusual in that. We had the same thing during the last months of the war, and for a time afterward—

deserters from the army turned outlaw stopping people along the highways."

Holly, fanning herself with her hat, looked back at her mother. Mattie, eyes closed, was continuing to sleep. It was probably best, the girl thought; she didn't seem to notice the heat and discomfort.

"I hope, for Mama's sake, that we don't run into any of them," Holly said.

Gannon nodded. "It could have been just talk," he said, and brushed at the sweat on his heavily lined face. A fair-skinned man, he had cold, blue eyes, light hair, and salt-and-pepper beard and mustache. His shoulders stirred.

"Hard to get used to not seeing anybody. Man can travel for hours—even days—in this country and never see a soul. Don't know if I can ever get used to that. Back in Pennsylvania—"

"That banker you dealt with in Carlisle said that Wickenburg was a fairly large town, and there are several other settlements in Arizona—some even larger. There'll be people there, Papa—a lot of them. Do you know if there are any mountains nearby, or is it in the plains country, like this?"

Gannon mopped at his brow with the back of a hand. The heat was becoming intense despite a faint breeze. "I never bothered to ask, but being a mining town I'd suspect it's in the mountains—or close to some."

"I hope so. I remember from school that Arizona was once the western half of New Mexico. That led me to think we'd find the same kind of country there —plains like we've been crossing."

"There are mountains in New Mexico," Gannon

said, gesturing toward the west where a formation of gray-blue, blurred by distance, lay upon the horizon.

"It really wouldn't matter much," Holly said, looking out over the flats and the low, rolling hills. "The plains are pretty in a wild sort of way. I've noticed patches of wild flowers, and now and then there are groves of trees."

"Compared to Pennsylvania it's barren," Gannon said flatly. "I wonder if—"

"Cheer up, Papa!" Holly broke in with a laugh. "We'll come to love Arizona just like we did Pennsylvania, and everything will work out just fine— you'll see."

9

"I sure don't want you thinking all the wagons we jump are like that one," Rooster said as he and Matt, riding side by side, struck off in the wake of Hooker and Fargo Smith, now only dark shapes in the distance. "Just happened Cud picked a poor one this time."

"Sort of got that idea from what was said," Buckman murmured.

"I feel kind of sorry for them folks," Rooster continued. "Was pure bad luck they happened along when they did. Expect Cud would've passed them up if there'd been another wagon somewheres in sight—or it hadn't been for the woman. She was a real looker—one of them big yellow-haired gals. Sure can't blame Cud much for—"

"There was no need to kill them," Matt said, repeating his earlier words.

"Maybe not if we hadn't stopped them, but once we'd done that I reckon there wasn't nothing else to do. We sure couldn't have them blabbing their guts out to the first jasper they run across."

Drumm paused, looked closely at Matt. "You best change your thinking about us and what we do for a living, because it sure won't be healthy if you don't.

And like I told you before, be mighty careful when you talk to Cud."

Buckman shrugged. "Habit of mine, I reckon, to say what I think—"

"Best you sort of pull in your horns, change that. It don't take much jawing to set Cud off, and if he got the notion that you ain't going along with us and what we do, and maybe are aiming to pull out, well, first thing you know you'd find yourself getting dirt thrown in your face somewhere along the trail like them pilgrims."

Rooster was silent for a long minute and then again faced Matt. "You ain't figuring on that, are you?"

Buckman shrugged. "Sure finding it hard to get used to," he said, avoiding the question as much as possible. "Punched cows most all of my life. Making a living this way sure is different."

Rooster laughed. "That's sure a fact! But you won't never be sorry. Can make more money in a day than you do in a month cowboying—twice as much sometimes."

"You plan to keep on doing this all the rest of your life?"

"Why not?" Rooster asked. "Leastwise I aim to until I get myself a poke full enough so's I won't have to do no work atall."

Drumm scrubbed at his jaw and grinned. "That'll be a long time coming, I expect. When we went to Denver to sell off the stuff a few months back I blowed every copper I had, and right now I'm dead, flat busted. But I ain't complaining. Had me one hell of a big time. It was worth every bit I spent."

"You think we'll be going to Denver or one of them other towns soon?"

"Probably. We've got enough hides now to make it look good."

"Look good?"

"Yeh, you know what I mean. Big thing we've got to sell and that brings in the money is the silverware and jewelry we've took off the pilgrims we stopped. Dealing in hides is just a way to keep the law from getting nosy and catching on to what we're really doing. . . . I reckon we'll be going to Dodge City this time. Cud figures it ain't smart to go to the same town twice in a row."

Matt pulled off his hat and swiped at the sweat on his forehead. "There a lot of silver and jewelry in the wagon?"

"Pretty fair pile. It's in that box up front, just back of the seat. Got hides piled on top of it. Some cash there, too. That's how Cud does it. Puts everything we get, cash and all, in that box so's it can be split even Stephen between us. Ain't never no cheating done. . . . Didn't I hear you say you was headed for Dodge when them Kiowas jumped you?"

Matt nodded. "Aimed to sign on with some rancher shipping a herd to Chicago."

"Well, I don't know how much money you'd draw doing that but I'm betting it ain't nowheres near what you'll be making now."

Buckman considered Rooster Drumm thoughtfully. "All that killing and robbing—don't that bother you some?"

Rooster shook his head. "Just don't ever think

much on it," he replied, frowning. "Why? It bother you?"

Caution once again came to the fore in Matt Buckman. He had already made a couple of bad mistakes, at least to the rawhiders' way of thinking, and he'd best tread carefully henceforth if he expected to get away from them alive.

"Something else that's going to take some getting used to," he said. "Got to own up to that."

"You will," Rooster said firmly. "Just like the stink of them hides, a man gets to where he don't even notice it. Looks like Cud and Fargo've pulled up—"

Matt raised his eyes and gazed ahead. Hooker had come to a halt at the edge of a small stand of trees and was climbing down from the seat. Nearby Fargo Smith was tieing his horse to one of the wagon's wheels.

"It's a mite early to be making camp—"

"Misdoubt we are," Rooster said with a shake of his head. "Cud's mighty careful. He'll be figuring it's too close to that wagon we just set afire and will want to keep going, put a few miles between us and it in case the soldiers or the law comes along. If we ain't nowheres around they can't ask us no questions."

"Expect those arrows you scattered around the clearing will make anybody stopping to see what happened think it was an Indian raid—"

"I reckon they do: leastwise we ain't never had nobody point a finger at us yet."

Rooster had been right about Cud Hooker. When he and Matt rode up and dismounted the rawhider was crouched beside the small creek flowing along the cottonwoods washing the crusted blood from his hands and arms. Upstream a few paces Fargo Smith was doing likewise.

"Matt was wondering if you aimed to camp here for the night," Rooster said as he hunched beside Hooker. "Told him I misdoubted it, that you'd figure it was too close to that wagon."

Cud, water dripping from his arms and hands, came to his feet and faced Drumm. "You done everything you was supposed to, didn't you?"

"Sure—sure did—"

"You seen to it that everything got burned, didn't you? And then you flung some of them arrows around so's it'd look like the Kiowas done it?"

"Sure did, Cud. Even stuck one in the old man."

Hooker bobbed. "Just wanted to be sure."

"Hell!" Rooster declared in an injured tone. "I ain't never fell down on doing my part yet, have I?"

"Nope, I reckon you ain't, but a man can get kind of careless and forget something once in a while, and when that happens he ain't no use no more. It's like an old spavined horse. Ain't nothing a fellow can do but shoot him."

Matt felt Hooker's small, agate-hard eyes drilling into him. The last of what the rawhider had said was probably for his benefit, he guessed, and he supposed he should make it appear as if he were suitably impressed.

"Rooster was right careful, Cud—both of us were," he said. "Did everything the way he said you wanted."

Again Hooker nodded and then, turning, started

toward the wagon. "No, we ain't camping here," he said as if suddenly remembering Rooster Drumm's words. "Aim to dig around in that hayshaker's grub box, see what I can find for us to eat without having to do any cooking. Then we'll head on west."

"West?" Fargo echoed. "How far?"

Hooker lifted the box of foodstuff taken from the pilgrim out of the wagon and set it on the ground. Crouching beside it he began to paw through its contents.

"Oh, for a couple of days, no more'n that. Pickings are too easy along this part of the trail to move on, and with them renegade Indians running loose around here to blame it on, we've got us a right good deal. . . . You all come over here and find yourself something to fill your belly with," he added, unscrewing the cap on a Mason jar containing some kind of preserved meat. "We won't be stopping to eat again for quite a spell."

It was as Cud Hooker told them: they moved on within the half hour, and although a halt was called around midnight there was no campfire and no cooking. The next morning Hooker did permit the making of coffee but once more ruled out any cooking, explaining that they would hold off until evening before stopping and setting up camp.

Following that plan a fire was built, a pot of coffee brewed, and cups filled and drunk hastily, after which they continued on west, somewhat to the right of but always within sight of the trail. On the third day Hooker began to veer due east. He had chosen to drive the wagon again, frankly admitting that his few short hours in the saddle had turned his thighs sore and his back lame—for which Matt Buckman was truly grateful. Astride Penmon's sorrel he could stay well away from the rank odor of the hides that filled the canvas-topped vehicle.

They crossed over the trail to its opposite side and began to double back into the direction from which they had come. Around midafternoon they spotted three wagons moving slowly toward them. Hooker, studying them intently through the glass, reported that they offered little hope of profit as the wagons were old and appeared broken-down, and he doubted there was fifty dollars in cash among the lot. Thus they were allowed to continue unmolested.

When the pilgrims had passed out of sight in the low, rolling hills, the rawhiders resumed their course, keeping now to the right of the rutted road. They halted near dark at the base of a red-faced bluff and made a dry camp. They had scarcely gotten the evening meal out of the way when Fargo, off to the side with the picketed horses where he was working on his black, which was showing signs of lameness, called out suddenly.

"Cud! Somebody coming on the trail!"

Hooker immediately brought out his telescope and trained it on the advancing rider. He held the glass on the man for several minutes, and then turned to Matt and Rooster.

"It's a goddammed lawman. Can see his star. Now, you two just go on about what you're doing, and keep your lip buttoned. I'll do all the talking. . . . Fargo, I reckon you know where you best be."

Hope lifted within Matt Buckman. A lawman!

This could mean his chance to break free of the rawhiders and put a stop to their murderous activities along the trail as well. All he need do was draw the man aside, quickly tell him what he had witnessed since Hooker and the others had saved him from the renegade Kiowas. For proof of such the lawman had only to look under the hides piled in the back of the wagon.

Hunkered near the fire with Rooster Drumm, Matt watched Fargo draw his pistol, thumb open the loading gate, and spin the cylinder while he checked the loads in the weapon. Satisfied the gun was ready for instantaneous use, the rawhider sauntered over to a nearby cottonwood and, with the pistol still in his hand, sat down. Folding his arms across his chest to effectively conceal the weapon, he settled back against the tree.

Matt swore silently. He could forget doing any talking to the lawman. If he made the slightest move to warn the man he'd be signing a death warrant for him as well as one for himself.

10

The lawman, a narrow-faced individual with dark eyes and a clipped mustache, rode into the center of the camp and pulled to a halt. Lean, dressed in a dusty, sun-faded brown suit, rumpled white shirt, black string tie, and a high-crowned, wide-brimmed hat that looked much too large for him, he dismounted without invitation and put his sharp attention on Hooker.

"Name's John Wingert, U.S. deputy marshal. You're—?"

"Cud Hooker. My partners here are—"

"This your outfit?"

"I reckon you could say so. These here fellows are my partners, howsomever."

"How long have you been in this area?"

"Oh, a week, maybe ten days. Why? What's the trouble, Marshal?"

Wingert drew a charred pipe from the left-hand pocket of his coat, knocked the dottle from its bowl by striking it against the heel of his boot, and began to refill it from a near-empty leather pouch.

"Got complaints about wagons being stopped along the trail, folks robbed, women bothered. You know anything about it?"

"Sure don't, except we did come across a wagon

up the trail a piece a few days back that sure had run into trouble. Found a man and a woman dead, and their outfit set afire. Indians, we figured—Kiowas or Comanches, ain't sure which."

"Rode by there myself a couple of days ago," Wingert said, lighting his pipe. His eyes never ceased moving, continually swept the camp, missing nothing. "Was you that skinned out those horses, I expect."

"Yes, sir, it was. They was laying there dead, and hides is our business, the way we make a living. Was no use letting them go to waste."

Wingert's shuttered gaze had halted on Fargo Smith. "What about the folks that were in the wagon?"

"Was two of them, a man and a woman. We buried them side by side. Only decent thing to do."

Wingert nodded, shifted his eyes to Matt and then to Rooster Drumm while puffing thoughtfully on his pipe.

"When did you say this happened?" he asked.

Hooker frowned, clawed at his beard. It was some cleaner now since the day they had halted beside a creek and he'd washed the blood of the pilgrims' two horses from his hands and arms.

"Well, I ain't no great shakes at remembering, but seems to me it was about a week ago. We was heading west looking for some stray cattle that we'd heard was running loose in the brush over there a ways. Never did find them so we started back up the trail—"

"Was wondering about that," Wingert broke in, taking the pipe from his mouth.

"About what?" Cud said affably.

"That wagon you're talking about getting burned up by the Indians is maybe twenty-five miles or more on up the trail. I find you headed up that way. Puzzled me how you could have been clear up there, and still be down here going back up that way."

Hooker laughed. "Done told you how it was, Marshal. We come down the trail hunting them steers, and now we're doubling back. In this here hide-hunting business a man has to keep on the move."

"Expect so," Wingert murmured, and again let his thoughtful glance touch Matt and Rooster Drumm and drift on to Fargo Smith sitting hunched and silent against the trunk of the cottonwood, arms still folded across his chest. "There enough money in hides to keep all four of you?"

"Bellies get flat sometimes," Cud said with a shake of his head, "but times are mighty hard everywhere. We get by the best we can."

"Been that way ever since the war ended," Wingert agreed. "I ain't so sure it's Indians doing the robbing and killing around here. You seen any riders other than them around?"

"Nope, nothing but a couple of bunches of Indians—Kiowas or Comanches. I ain't never been able to tell the difference."

"The arrows I found up around that wagon—or what was left of it—were Kiowa."

Wingert's pipe had gone out. Reaching into a pocket of his vest the lawman procured a match, fired it with a thumbnail, and puffed the briar into life again.

"One thing keeps bothering me," he said, eyes on

Hooker. "Indians don't usually fool with keepsake things the way white folks do—silverware, jewelry boxes, metal doodads and such—but I've never found any trace of things like that around the burnt-up wagons I've come across."

"Expect the fire would've taken care of everything."

"Not everything. I figure there still ought to be some melted-down silver or lead in the ashes, maybe even some cash. Ain't never anything like that."

Hooker's rough features had drawn into a knot. "Marshal, way you're talking it sounds like there's been other pilgrims killed and robbed, like them poor folks back up the trail—"

"There has," Wingert said, puffing slowly on his briar. He had never removed his cold, speculative gaze from Hooker.

"And you're thinking that maybe it ain't them renegade Indians doing it?" Cud said, surprise in his tone.

"I am—"

Hooker pulled off his hat, wagged his head. "Well, I'll be good goddammed! I just can't figure white men doing things like that to other white men and their women. No, sir, I sure can't."

Wingert made no comment but continued to suck at his pipe. The buckskin horse he was riding looked worn and was covered with sweat-caked trail dust, as was the gear on his broad back, Matt noticed. Evidently the lawman had been on the move for some time.

"A renegade's a renegade no matter whether he's

white, red, or black," the lawman said. "You men for sure you ain't seen nobody around but them Kiowas?"

Both Matt and Rooster shook their heads. Fargo Smith only shrugged. Cud set his hat back on his head, and scrubbed at his wiry beard.

"That's all, Marshal, excepting folks traveling on the trail. Was three wagons passed by this morning —or maybe it was yesterday. Sure do have a hard time remembering things nowadays."

"I saw them, too," Wingert said. "Told them to keep a sharp eye. . . . You mind if I have a look in your wagon?"

The tension that had hung over the camp since the lawman's arrival suddenly increased. Rooster drew himself slowly erect and assumed a carefully slouched position. Fargo Smith stirred slightly. Cud Hooker's manner—easygoing and friendly—remained the same.

"Why sure, Marshal; just help yourself. You ain't going to find nothing but hides—a pretty fair stack of them. We're aiming to keep on going east this time till we hit Dodge. Figure to sell them off there."

Wingert, knocking the tobacco from his pipe, and returning it to a pocket, cast a side glance at Fargo, and then at Rooster and Matt, crossed slowly to the wagon, and halted at the tailgate. The expression on his weathered face altered visibly when the nauseating odor of the hides greeted him.

"Just you climb right in; it won't hurt nothing," Hooker said. "Ain't going to find nothing but hides, but I reckon you've got to be sure."

Wingert drew his pistol and with its barrel lifted a corner of the top horsehide. The movement disturbed a host of flies and apparently released a heavy wave of the sickening stench. The lawman stepped back quickly and holstered his weapon.

"You want some help, Marshal?" Cud offered.

Wingert shook his head, and drawing his bandanna from a hip pocket mopped at his face. "No, I reckon I've seen enough."

Rooster Drumm smiled. "He sure said the right thing there. If he'd dug a little deeper he'd found two or three gunnysacks underneath the pile—all filled with silverware and stuff we been collecting."

"What about the box that's up front—the one with the cash and jewelry in it?" Matt asked.

"Reckon he couldn't see it from the tail end of the wagon," Rooster murmured, and glanced at Fargo. Smith had not changed his position against the trunk of the tree and was continuing to watch the lawman with sharp interest. "If that tin star had made one wrong move—like climbing up into the wagon, or digging down under them hides—he'd be a dead man right now."

Matt got to his feet. "Killing a lawman, specially a U.S. marshal—that's mighty bad business."

"Wouldn't make no difference to Fargo or Cud. If they figure somebody needs killing, why, hell, they kill him."

Wingert had moved away from the rear of the wagon and was walking slowly back into the center of the camp. Matt, still hoping desperately for an opportunity to talk to the lawman, gave it up. John Wingert hadn't realized it but with Fargo Smith,

Hooker, and Rooster Drumm ready to turn on him at the slightest provocation, he had been treading on thin ice from the moment he rode up.

"You say you're moving on to Dodge City?" the lawman said, halting beside the weary buckskin.

"Sure am—ain't sure when we'll get there. We'll be scouting around for hides while we're on the way, but that's where we figure to end up."

Wingert grasped the reins and the saddle horn and drew himself stiffly up and into the well-worn old hull.

"I'm obliged to you for your time, Hooker," he said glancing about, "even to your partners there, who've lost their tongues. I'll tell you what I told those pilgrims: best you keep a sharp eye out. Whoever's pirating folks along this trail ain't to be fooled with."

Cud nodded. "We're obliged to you, Marshal, for warning us, but I don't figure they'll bother us. We ain't got nothing nobody would want."

"Your horses—those renegade Kiowas would take a shine to them. . . . That's something else that keeps nagging at me—why they killed that team —the one you skinned out a few days back."

"They wasn't worth nothing," Hooker said with a shake of his head. "Real poor stock—old, half starved. They wouldn't be no good to a Indian."

"Guess you're right," Wingert said after a moment, and, touching the brim of his hat with a forefinger, rode out of camp.

11

Fargo Smith came to his feet slowly, his flat gaze on the departing lawman. Pistol still in hand, the rawhider hooked his thumb over the cocked hammer of the weapon and let it slip back into the safety notch.

Hooker, also watching the marshal, swore deeply. "That jasper was a mite nosy—dang nigh too nosy."

"I was ready for him," Fargo said in that cool, positive way of his, and then glanced at Matt. "Did you have something on your mind—maybe something you wanted to tell that badge toter?"

A tautness gripped Buckman. Evidently his hope to get a message across to John Wingert had somehow shown through. Mustering a half grin he shook his head at the rawhider, aware in that same moment that Rooster had pulled back a step or two from him and that Cud Hooker was staring at him through narrowed, hard-surfaced eyes.

"What the hell would I be wanting to tell him?" Matt demanded harshly.

Fargo, weapon hanging loosely at his side, thumb again on the hammer, hawked and spat into the dust. "I don't know. You tell me."

"Nothing to tell," Matt said evenly. "You're seeing things, Fargo."

Smith was silent for a long breath and then, sliding his gun back into the holster, shrugged. "Maybe."

"Now hold on," Hooker said, cutting in. "We best get to the bottom of this right now. You see Buckman trying to high-sign that marshal, Fargo?"

Smith shook his head. "No, nothing like that. Just sort of looked like he wanted to."

Hooker snorted in disgust and turned to Rooster. "You was standing there with him. You see him do anything to draw that law dog's attention?"

"Nope, can't say as I did," Rooster replied. "Me and him was right here together all the time, and I sure don't see how he could have give the marshal any high sign without me catching on."

Cud Hooker folded his thick arms across his chest and considered Matt coldly. "I reckon there weren't nothing to it, but you best hear this. There ain't no room in my outfit for a backstabber, and if one ever turns up he can sure figure himself a dead man right then and there. You savvy that?"

Matt nodded. He had suddenly found himself backed into a corner, and it looked for a few minutes as if there were no out. In some way he had aroused Fargo Smith's suspicions. The rawhider had then in turn passed the thought on to Cud— even to Rooster Drumm, who had been more or less his friend. But he'd managed to work his way into the clear—at least for the time being.

"If you catch me double-crossing you," he said with a wry grin at Hooker, "you've got my permission to fill me full of lead. Goes for all of you."

Rooster laughed, breaking the tension. "Well now, that's a mighty fine offer—one I'm sure hoping

I won't have to ever take you up on," he said, and as Hooker walked away he continued: "We camping here tonight, Cud?"

"Aim to move on," the rawhider said. "You and Buckman get that grub box and stuff loaded in the wagon, and we'll pull out. I don't want to be in the same place in case that marshal comes back looking for us on some excuse or other."

Fargo, crossing to his horse, agreed. "Just what I was thinking. Something about that tin star I don't trust."

Relieved to be out from under the taut pressure of suspicion, Matt moved over to the grub box and began to collect the pans and other articles they had made use of and stowed them in the container. Rooster joined him at his chores and shortly they were loaded.

"You want me to drive the wagon?" Matt asked as Hooker passed nearby.

"I'll do it. You ride the horse," the rawhider answered.

They headed out immediately after that, Hooker with Fargo Smith alongside the wagon, leading the way, while Matt and Rooster Drumm brought up the rear. It was full dark a time later when Cud pulled off the trail and halted, a mile or so farther on, in a welter of low hills and bluffs through which a wide, sandy arroyo cut its way.

"There ain't no creek around," Hooker said as he came off the wagon. "Have to use some of the water in the barrel for the horses."

"We're getting low," Rooster commented.

"Can fill up tomorrow at that spring that's on up

the way about ten or twelve mile. . . . Ain't no
need for a fire," he added, glancing at Matt.

Buckman tossed aside the sticks he was collecting. "Figured somebody'd be wanting coffee—"

"They can wait till morning," the rawhider said
bluntly. Evidently he was still thinking about John
Wingert and the possibility that the glow of the fire,
seen from the trail, could draw him.

"Sure all right with me," Matt said.

He started to add that he was already sick of being
camp cook and would as soon someone else took
over the chore, but thought better of it. His place
with the rawhiders was none too secure as it was,
thanks to Fargo Smith; for the next few days it
would be wise to watch carefully what he said or did.

The night was bright and, although they were in
the high plains country, somewhat warm. Hunched
against the foot of a low cut, a brown paper ciga-
rette—courtesy of Rooster Drumm, who shared his
sack of Bull Durham and fold of tissue wrappers
with him—dangling from the corner of his mouth,
Matt tried again as he had a dozen times before to
figure a way to leave, actually escape, from Cud
Hooker and his rawhiders.

He had considered taking the sorrel horse that
had belonged to Penmon, the man killed by the
Indians, and making a run for it when he had an
opportunity. But the odds of getting away with that
were very small; doubtless Hooker, and especially
Fargo Smith, would now be watching him closely.

Matt reckoned the smart thing to do was to stop
raking his brain for a plan and just sit tight. Hooker
had said they would be going on to Dodge City for

the purpose of selling off the hides and the booty they had collected. Such would afford the opportunity he needed to break away from them. In a town the size of Dodge it wouldn't be difficult to slip away, and if he still felt it was the right thing to do, he could go to the law and tell what he knew about Cud Hooker and his partners.

Matt swore softly. *The right thing to do!* Hell, he was getting as bad as they were—questioning something like that. All three of them were killers, cold-blooded murderers; there could be no question as to what was right and wrong. He was bound by all that was decent to report them to the law.

Apparently John Wingert had continued on his way west, as the night passed without event. Not long after daylight Matt, still unable to break the habit of rising early, was up and about preparing the morning meal. He did so as quietly as possible, and when Hooker and the others finally turned out, he had an intentionally good meal of fried potatoes, bacon from the grub box of the pilgrims' wagon, sliced onion, also from the larder of the luckless traveler, warm bread spread with butter, coffee, and canned peaches ready for them.

Fargo Smith made no comment on the unusually tasty breakfast but Hooker expressed his appreciation by wiping his hands across his thick lips and then, Indian fashion, giving his belly a hearty slap.

"Now, eats like that sure sets a man up for a good day's work!" he declared. "And I got the feeling that's just what we're in for—a lot of real fine luck a-smiling down at us. . . . What say we get started?"

They were off and moving east within the hour, this time with Matt driving the wagon and Cud Hooker once again in the saddle riding out ahead with Fargo and Rooster flanking him. No more had been said about U.S. Deputy Marshal Wingert, and Matt hoped it was now behind him and soon to be forgotten, but of that he was unsure where Fargo Smith was concerned. Several times he caught the burly rawhider studying him thoughtfully as if striving to determine one way or another where he stood.

Around noon the riders ahead of him came to a halt. Matt saw the glint of sunlight on Hooker's brass telescope as he viewed something far up the trail. The rawhider continued to consider whatever it was that had drawn his attention for a long five minutes, and then abruptly all wheeled and returned to where Matt had stopped.

"Want you to pull off there behind that brush," Hooker said to Matt, pointing to a thicket a dozen yards off the trail. "We got us a jim-dandy a-coming, and I don't want nothing scaring them and getting them all worked up."

"What is it?" Matt asked.

"Real fine wagon and team. Man and a woman on the seat—young woman."

"I'm thinking about that," Fargo drawled. "You been getting first grabs on the women right along. I figure it's about my turn."

Hooker frowned, stared at Smith. After a bit his shoulders stirred. "This here looks like a prize little filly, but I reckon we can hash out who gets her later. . . . Now, Buckman, you stay put there in the brush. When you hear us shooting, come a-running. With that dang marshal somewheres around, we'll have to do our doings fast, and then get the hell out of here."

Rooster hesitated as he was about to turn away. "Maybe it'd be smart to pass up this one, Cud—just in case that lawman is dogging us."

"Not this one—no, sir!" Hooker declared emphatically. "Worth taking a chance on because this here's a rich one. I'll bet the old geezer driving that team of duns has got a whole bucketful of double eagles in his wagon!"

12

Matt Buckman, standing off to one side of the wagon, watched the rawhiders ride out. As soon as they had rounded a spur of trees and brush along the trail he pivoted and, moving into the open, scanned the country to the west. There was a chance that John Wingert, the U.S. marshal, was still around. He hadn't appeared too satisfied with what he saw in Hooker's camp, and just maybe could be keeping an eye on the rawhiders.

But there was no sign of the lawman. Matt then considered the idea of climbing into the wagon and heading on west in the hope that he would overtake Wingert—but that would be a big gamble, and the odds would all be against him. The marshal would be far down the trail by that hour—and there was no real assurance that he had continued on west; he could have swung southeast for Texas or he could have veered north with the intention of going to Colorado. Too, Matt realized that everything would depend on his joining up with the marshal quickly as Hooker and his partners, guessing what he had in mind when they saw their wagon moving off into the opposite direction to instructions, would give chase and, on horseback, very quickly catch up with the slower vehicle.

Coming about Matt retraced his steps to the wagon and settled down on a rock nearby—but at a respectable distance from the foul-smelling hides. He had no idea of how long he'd have to wait; the bend in the trail hid the rawhiders from sight; thus there was no way of knowing if they were one mile or five away.

Abruptly two gunshots sounded. Matt got to his feet and crossed to the wagon and swung up onto the seat. More shots echoed flatly in the still, hot air as he gathered up the lines, wheeled the team about and turned onto the trail.

As he rounded the finger of brush and scrub trees Buckman saw the pilgrim wagon with Hooker, Fargo, and Rooster Drumm racing alongside—but at a safe distance. A woman was driving the canvas-topped vehicle. She was leaning forward, lines clutched in one hand, while she plied the whip with the other. With her on the seat was an elderly man, rifle at his shoulder, firing steadily at the rawhiders. The wagon, pulled by a fine-looking pair of horses, was swaying from side to side and several times rocked so wildly that Buckman thought it would go over.

Matt slowed to meet the oncoming rawhiders and the pilgrims. Through the haze of dust he saw Fargo abruptly ride in close to the driver's side of the wagon. The man, standing partly upright as he levered his rifle, suddenly stiffened and dropped the weapon. The woman, very young, Matt saw as he got a closer look, tried to snatch up the rifle while still handling the team. At that moment Cud

Hooker appeared in the arch of canvas behind her, having entered the wagon from its rear.

His bulking shape was silhouetted briefly in the opening, and then he reached forward, seized the reins the woman was holding. Wrenching them from her grasp, he brushed her roughly aside, and hauling back on the lines brought the team to a walk.

Immediately Hooker swung the horses about, and beckoning for Matt to follow drove the wagon off the trail and into a cluster of trees a hundred yards or so to the right. Fargo Smith and Rooster Drumm remained in the roadway, their eyes searching the surrounding country for signs of anyone who might have witnessed the incident, and then as Hooker brought the wagon to a stop they hurriedly rejoined him, arriving there at about the same moment as Matt.

"Cut in close!" Hooker shouted to Buckman, and motioned to a place alongside the pilgrims' vehicle —a well-known brand that had been specially reinforced and equipped for the long journey its owner had planned to make. The team also was of the best —a pair of husky, spirited dun geldings—and Matt quickly realized why the rawhiders had preferred to run down the horses rather than shoot them; Cud Hooker no doubt intended to appropriate the span for his own use.

"Get cracking!" Hooker, quickly on the ground, ordered. Reaching up he dragged the woman, one no more than eighteen or nineteen, Matt judged, off the seat and down to his side. "Aim to get away from here fast!"

At that moment the girl wrenched free of Hooker's grasp. Whirling about, she started into the trees, then came to an abrupt halt as she ran squarely into Fargo Smith. The big rawhider, grinning broadly with pleasure, gathered her slight figure into his muscular arms and drew her close.

"I sure got me a prize here—one worth more'n a whole wagonload of buffalo hides!" he declared, crushing her to his barrel-like chest.

The girl screamed, struggled to break away, but Fargo's grip about her was like a vise. Her dark hair had come down as she fought to free herself, and her eyes, Matt saw when she turned partly toward him, were a light blue and for the moment were bright with terror.

"Ain't no time for that now," Hooker said, shaking his head as if disapproving Smith's actions. "Best we get done what needs doing, and then pull out of here."

Fargo glared at Hooker, head thrust forward, eyes narrowed, thick shoulders bulging with muscles. Smith had once felled a horse with a single blow of his hamlike fist, Rooster had told Matt, and had strength enough to overturn a wagon.

"I ain't turning her loose till me and you gets something settled," Fargo stated sullenly. "This here gal's mine. You ain't getting first dibs on her like you been doing lately with them others. I'll—"

Hooker, gaze fastened upon the girl's straining shapely figure, shook his head. "I reckon we'll decide that when we're done," he said, and beckoned to Matt. "Come on over here and grab onto her. Best tie her up to something—one of the wagon wheels'll be best. There's some rawhide cord under the seat."

Fargo reluctantly surrendered the girl to Matt, who took a firm grip on a wrist. She was gasping for breath and he could feel her trembling violently.

"You let her get away and I'll skin you alive," Smith warned in a harsh voice.

Matt made no reply but led the girl off to the rawhider's wagon. Holding tight to her he reached into the bed, located a length of leather string, and, drawing the girl's hands together, bound them to a wheel.

"Rooster, you and Fargo lug the old man over there into the brush," Hooker directed, climbing up into the pilgrims' vehicle. "There's a dead woman in here—get her out. Can put her with him."

"What'll you be doing?" Fargo asked suspiciously as Rooster hastened to comply.

"I aim to start digging through all the stuff that's in here. Bound to be a sack of money somewheres." Cud paused as if suddenly realizing something. "Why? You getting big ideas in your head like I ain't running this outfit right no longer?"

Fargo spat, brushed his hat to the back of his head, and walked slowly up to the wagon, where Rooster was dragging the body of the man off the floorboards.

"Maybe. For sure I'm telling you I ain't much cottoning to the way things've been going lately. You been having everything your way—hogging it all."

"You been getting your full share of everything

ever since we throwed in together—and you'll keep
on getting it, even Stephen—every time we sell off."

"I aim to," Fargo said quietly; "can bet on that,"
and taking hold of the dead man by the shoulders
lifted him clear of the wagon. "Something else you
best get straight: I aim to have that girl. She's
mine."

"Damn it all, Fargo, what's got into you?" Hooker
demanded, exploding suddenly. "I said we'd talk
about it later! We going to jaw all afternoon about
her?" he added, picking up a leather wallet filled
with papers that had dropped from the dead man's
pocket.

"Not needful long as you savvy how things
stand," Fargo replied. "I ain't putting up with you
doing like you did the other day. Was me that
should've had that big yellow-haired woman. Instead you just went right on ahead like I didn't have
no rights to nothing."

Hooker was ignoring Fargo Smith as he went
through the folded papers he had recovered. Glancing up after a few moments he put his glance on the
girl.

"Says here your name is Gannon—Holly Gannon. Your pa there was Caleb, and your ma was
called Mattie. Ain't that right?"

The girl, still trembling although her frantic
breathing had subsided, made no answer. Hooker
grinned, glanced at Fargo and Rooster Drumm,
now carrying the body of the man off into the brush.

"Well, Holly Gannon, it don't make no never-
mind to me who you are. You'll talk when I want you
to: can make up your mind to that."

Holly's shoulders came up into a square line and a defiance filled her eyes. She was pretty, Matt thought, and a wave of pity washed over him as he realized what lay ahead for her at the hands of Fargo Smith or Cud Hooker—whichever one finally claimed her. He wished that he might in some way help her and—

"Buckman, get me one of them gunnysacks, bring it over here," Hooker shouted as he drew himself over the back of the seat and into the rear of the wagon. "That gal don't need looking after. She ain't going nowhere if you tied her up good."

Matt turned, obtained a burlap bag from several under the seat, and started to comply with the rawhider's order. The girl suddenly broke and began to weep. Glancing off to the side Buckman saw Fargo and Rooster now carrying the body of a woman—Holly's mother, he assumed—over to where they had laid Caleb Gannon. He glanced at her, wishing there were something he could say to comfort her. Holly caught him looking. Anger blazed in her tear-filled eyes.

"You—you murderers!" she stormed. "You're worse than—than animals!"

Matt shook his head. He wished he could say something to Holly Gannon, make her understand his position, but there was no opportunity.

"Buckman, damn it—get the hell over here!" Hooker shouted impatiently.

Matt immediately pivoted. Fargo, apparently having gone through the pockets of Caleb Gannon and collected what money the man was carrying, slowed as he moved toward the pilgrims' wagon and stared at Matt.

"Don't you go getting any hankerings for that gal," he snapped. "She's mine."

Matt continued on, paying no mind to Smith. He would like it very much if he could help Holly, but he could think of no way. Hell, he couldn't even help himself get free of the rawhiders!

Shock and disbelief gripped Holly Gannon. That this could be happening to her, to her mother and father, was beyond all comprehension. Sick from the terrible odor emanating from the wagon to which she was tied, and from the outlaws, fighting to control the paralyzing fear and grief that was all but overwhelming her, she sagged against the wheel that the one called Buckman had lashed her to and watched the four men go about the literal destruction of her family.

It had been the Indians her father feared, Holly was remembering. Renegades he had called them that lay in wait along the trail and attacked passing travelers as they made their way west. These weren't Indians; these were white men, she thought bitterly, outlaws of the very worst kind, and she couldn't be much worse off if it had been renegade Indians who had set upon them, killing both her mother and her father and now holding her prisoner.

She wondered about her mother. Had she died from a bullet as had her father, or was it that in her precarious, weakened condition the strain and frenzy of those few minutes when they sought to escape had brought about her death? Holly hoped she had not suffered; she'd had enough of that during the last few years of her life.

Holly shuddered as the burly outlaw who had caught her when she had tried to run off into the woods paused to look at her with his small, pig eyes. She'd heard him arguing with the one in her folks' wagon over her. He seemed to be claiming her. *Claiming her!* It was as if she were some sort of prize in a filthy game they were playing, she thought, and began to struggle furiously against her rawhide bonds. After a few moments she gave in; it had accomplished nothing more than turn the flesh of her wrists raw.

A fresh wave of anger and indignation swept through Holly as she watched one of the men in the wagon pawing about in the family possessions. She saw a dull flash, realized he had found the silverware—heirlooms handed down through generations of her father's people—and was dumping them into the burlap sack the one named Buckman had provided. Other articles were going into the sack, too; anything and everything that would bring a price somewhere would be included, she supposed.

The man inside the wagon paused to say something to Buckman and the other younger man. A short time later she saw the pair, one with a shovel, the other carrying her mother's patch quilt, move off toward the thicket of brush where she had seen them take the bodies of her parents. They were going to bury her folks—not properly but by simply digging a trench and putting them into it without any thought as to what they were really doing: marking the end on earth of two lives. Sobs again racking her body, Holly renewed her attack on the rawhide cord locking her to the wheel, but as before to no avail.

Exhausted, she fell back against her iron and spoked prison. She supposed she should be grateful for the burial they were getting. She'd heard tales of how bodies of those who died or were killed during their travels were simply left along the trail or out on the prairie for the great broad-winged vultures she'd seen soaring overhead to take care of. At least her mother and father would not be subjected to that.

Now she must think of herself, concentrate, come up with a means for escape. They were both beyond any earthly help, and it was clear what was ahead for her in the brutal hands of the four outlaws. She must get away, and perhaps she could if she bided her time until they released her. Then she might have a chance to get her hands on a knife, or maybe even a gun—preferably the former as she'd had no experience using a firearm—and if she failed in an attempt to escape she could use the weapon on herself.

The outlaws would show her no mercy, of that Holly was certain.

13

"You and Rooster get rid of them two stiffs," Hooker said as he took the sack from Matt. "Don't forget stringing a few of them arrows around. Want this to look like it was them renegade Kiowas that done it, same as before."

Buckman stepped back, made way for Fargo Smith to climb up into the wagon. Hooker shifted his attention to him.

"You find any cash on the old man?"

"About forty dollars, along with a turnip watch worth maybe two or three cartwheels. How about you?" Fargo asked, looking past his partner to where Holly Gannon was lashed to the rawhider's vehicle.

"Still digging. Got some silver doodads and a little jewelry. Got to be a sack of cash somewhere. The old man was a rich one; can tell by his rig and by the stuff he brought along."

"Sure fixed hisself up with a mighty tempting daughter," Fargo said, and laughed.

Matt turned away. Rooster, apparently having overheard Hooker, and now with the spade in one hand and half a dozen Kiowa arrows in the other, was already moving toward the brush where the bodies of Caleb and Mattie Gannon had been laid.

Buckman, ignoring Fargo Smith's jeering glance, picked up one of the quilts Hooker had pushed to the rear of the wagon and joined Rooster.

"Got to do this fast," Drumm said as Matt came up. "Cud's in an all-fired big hurry—on account of maybe that marshal showing up again. Reckon I'm a mite jumpy about him, too," he added and began to hollow out a trench alongside the two bodies.

"Didn't think it'd make any difference to Fargo, lawman or not," Matt said, wiping sweat off his forehead. "Way you talked I figured nothing would make him hold off."

"Ain't talking about Fargo, I'm talking about Cud. Things are a mite different with him. He looks at it kind of like you do—that killing a lawman can stir up a real passel of trouble."

"That's the truth," Matt said, crouching beside the body of Mattie Gannon. The faint glint of gold on a finger of her left hand had caught his eye. A wedding ring. Fargo had missed it somehow.

"I ain't digging this very deep," Rooster said. "Just enough to say we buried them in case we get asked. Anyway, them two, like old Fargo said, won't know the difference."

"No, guess they won't," Matt agreed. Slipping the small circle of gold off the woman's finger he tucked it into a pocket of his leather vest and took up the patchwork quilt and opened it. Rooster grinned at him.

"You're sure long on being nice to dead folks," he said dryly.

"Only being decent. You through digging?"

"Reckon so."

Matt spread the quilt over the trench, and then with Rooster's help laid the bodies side by side into it and drew the quilt into place to cover them. That done, Rooster immediately began to fill in the grave with loose soil.

"Maybe it'll be a good idea if we piled some rocks on top," Matt said, and walked to where a number of stones, apparently washed down from a higher level at some time in the past, caught his eye.

Rooster made no comment but continued to fill in the hollow as Buckman collected an armload of smooth rocks and brought them up to complete the burial. Over in the Gannon wagon the sounds of Hooker and Fargo Smith going through the possessions of the family could be heard. Matt could not see the girl from where he stood but knew she would be where he had left her—secured by a rawhide thong to the wheel of the rawhiders' vehicle. He wished again there were some way he could help her.

"Can throw them rocks on the grave now if you're of a mind," Matt heard Rooster say. "I ain't digging up no more dirt to throw on them."

Matt dropped the stones he'd gathered on the low mound, went back for a second load.

"You're wasting time," Drumm said gruffly. "We got plenty of other things to do—and if Cud or Fargo sees you they'll raise holy hell. . . . Anyways, you got enough rocks on top of that grave to keep the varmints out for a hundred years!"

Matt said nothing, simply went back to the accumulation of stones for another supply and added them to what he had placed on the grave.

"Expect that'll take care of it," he said, and reached for the spade. "I'll put this back on the wagon, you get rid of those arrows."

Rooster nodded his agreement, passed the tool to Matt, and moved off toward the Gannon wagon.

"Cud, you aiming to burn this rig or you going to do some swapping?" Matt heard Drumm ask as he halted at the tail gate of the vehicle.

"We ain't got the time to do that," Hooker responded. "Besides, somebody'd be sure to recognize a fine outfit like this. . . . You get done planting them two?"

"Sure did—"

"Then get busy scattering them arrows around. Make it look good. You stick one in that old man or woman?"

"Damn," Rooster said, "sure did forget that," Rooster muttered.

There was no reaction on Cud Hooker's part for several moments, and then he said: "Maybe that's just as well. Don't want it looking like a fixed-up job in case that two-bit marshal comes back and digs them up."

Rooster, obviously relieved, said, "Expect you're right, Cud, for sure. Now I'll start throwing these arrows here and there—aim to stick one in the side of the wagon."

"Yeh, just you do that, and soon as you're done get over there and keep an eye on the trail for that lawman. And tell Buckman to tote up some brush and pile it under this wagon so's it'll be ready to set afire."

"Good as done, Cud. You and Fargo having any luck in there?"

"Ain't found no money yet if that's what you mean. Turned up some silverware and jewelry, but there's cash in here somewheres, I know that for damn sure. This jasper was a prosperous gent of some kind."

"With this kind of an outfit I'm betting he was, too," Drumm said and went on about scattering the Kiowa arrows in the small clearing.

Matt Buckman, in the act of replacing the spade in its bracket on the side of the rawhiders' wagon, listened to the conversation that was taking place, hopeful of hearing something that would produce an idea for escape—not only for himself but for the girl. Brushing at the sweat misting his eyes, he swore softly. He had come up empty again. There still seemed no way.

The spade secure in its usual place, Matt circled the wagon to where the girl stood, head down, against the wheel of the vehicle. She glanced up, fear mounting swiftly in her eyes, as he halted before her.

"Want you to know I—" he began, but Holly cut him off.

"Get away from me—get away—you—you murderer!" she screamed in a voice trembling with hate.

Matt glanced toward the Gannon wagon. The two men inside could have heard the girl. Rooster Drumm did. He paused at his chore and looked questioningly toward Holly, but he had been lucky insofar as the rawhiders inside the wagon were concerned; there'd been no reaction there.

"Settle down," Matt said sternly, waving reassuringly at Rooster. "I aim to help you if I can. I'm not one of—"

"Go—get away from me! You hear? Get away!"

Holly screamed her words louder, frantic with fear, numbed by grief. Nothing Matt said had registered on her mind. His words had been meaningless.

"What the hell's going on out there?"

Fargo Smith's grating voice came from the front of the Gannon wagon. Matt turned to face him.

"Was being sure she wasn't getting loose," he said. "You about finished in there?"

Fargo glared at Matt for a long breath and then reached back into the interior of the vehicle and produced the burlap sack Matt had provided and tossed it to the ground.

"Yeh, far as I can see," he said. "Put this here sack of stuff in the wagon—under the hides. We ain't found no money yet."

Buckman retrieved the sack and did as Fargo had directed, all under the hating eyes of the girl. Abruptly Hooker and Smith came out of the wagon, Cud cursing angrily at their failure to turn up the cash he was certain Caleb Gannon had brought with him. Both men crouched and began to examine underneath the bed of the vehicle.

"Ain't no sign of a false bottom that I can see," Fargo said after a time.

"Weren't no sign of one on the top side either," Hooker said, continuing to check carefully the underfloor of the wagon bed. Five minutes later he gave it up. "There ain't none for damn sure," he declared and, eyes snapping, crossed to where the girl stood.

"All right, missy, I want to know where your pa hid his money! Wasn't on him, and me and Fargo couldn't find it in the wagon."

Holly, mustering courage, shook her head. "I don't know," she replied defiantly.

"I ain't about to believe that," Hooker said. "He'd a' told you, and guessing from that fine wagon and span of horses, he probably brought along a whole potful."

"I told you I don't know," Holly repeated, her voice breaking a little.

"And I'm telling you I don't swallow that," Cud stated flatly. "Now, you best make up your mind to speak up because I'll get it out of you one way or another—starting with peeling off your duds and seeing if you've got it hid on you somewheres."

"If there's any peeling done to her, I'll do it," Fargo said coldly, moving nearer to the girl. "Done staked my claim on her, so it's me that'll—"

"This here's business," Hooker snapped, and stepping up to Holly began to run his hands over her body in search of a money belt or any other means she might have employed to carry cash.

The girl flinched, struggled to pull away, but the leather cord kept her pinned to the wheel while the rawhider continued a methodical probing of her slender figure.

Fargo Smith, anger growing within him as he stood by and witnessed a procedure that he felt should have rightfully fallen to him, suddenly reached out, seized Hooker by the shoulder, and jerked him away from the girl.

"You're done looking for something on her—you're just having yourself a good time," he snarled. "I'm telling you to back off. Any more looking or stripping to be done, I'll be the one to do it!"

Hooker, slightly off balance, righted himself and squared around to face Fargo Smith. His broad features were taut with anger, and his right hand rested on the hilt of the knife hanging at his side.

"Just who the hell you think you are?" he demanded in a restrained, almost soft voice. "I'm running this outfit and you best own up to it right now."

Rooster Drumm, hurrying up from the rise where he had been keeping watch on the trail, thrust himself in between the two men, poised wire-taut, as they glared at each other.

"Hell, Cud, Fargo don't mean nothing by what he said. He's just wanting to be sure the gal—"

"Keep your goddammed nose out of this," Hooker broke in, his voice still quiet, and with a sweep of his thick arm brushed Drumm aside. "This here's been coming on for a long time and I aim to settle it here and now."

Matt, realizing what was imminent and that it likely represented his and the girl's one chance of escape from the rawhiders, eased himself along the side of the wagon to the rear where the saddle horses had been tied. Releasing the slip knots in the reins with a slight jerk, he freed the animals, which continued to doze in the warm sunlight. It would be better if they had taken it on themselves to wander off, but they had not, and he could not risk drawing the rawhiders' attention by driving them away himself. Quickly he returned to his place beside the girl. A hard grin pulled at his mouth. That much was done; now, if matters went as he hoped, the opportunity for escape would be at hand.

Fargo, his features a hard, cold mask, was shaking his head. "Expect you'll be making a mistake, Cud. Always wondered if you was big enough to take me. Right now I don't figure you are."

Matt drew his knife and, catching the girl's eye, cut the rawhide binding her to the wheel. "Don't move till I tell you," he murmured. "Then climb up into your pa's wagon fast as you can."

Holly stared at him, her eyes filled with mistrust and suspicion. "I—I don't understand. Why would you want to help me? You're one of them—no better or—"

"Suit yourself," Buckman replied, carefully keeping his voice down. "But if you want to get away from them you best do what I tell you."

Cud Hooker had moved farther out into the clearing. "I reckon this is the time to find out for sure about that," he said, and spinning abruptly drove a hard right into Fargo's jaw.

The blow connected with a sharp crack. Fargo staggered, went down. Dazed, he lay there motionless for a number of moments, and then, curses streaming from his thick lips, he lunged to his feet and threw himself on Hooker.

Matt glanced quickly at the girl. "Let's go," he said in a low, urgent voice.

14

Holly, either undergoing a change of attitude or grasping at straws, complied instantly. As Fargo Smith, arms outspread, head lowered, collided with Hooker, carrying the rawhider to the ground in a thrashing, flailing heap, she hurriedly crossed the narrow distance that lay between the two wagons and climbed up onto the seat of the one that had been her father's.

Matt, pistol in hand and moving equally swiftly, stepped up behind Rooster, back turned while he watched, fascinated, the struggle going on between the two men. Holding the weapon by the barrel, Buckman rapped Drumm sharply on the head with the butt. Rooster groaned and then sank quietly to the ground.

Throwing a quick look at Hooker and Smith, all but invisible in the haze of dust their scuffling had stirred up, Matt saw they were still too occupied with their own immediate problem to note what was happening elsewhere in the camp. Holstering his .45, Matt circled to the back of the rawhiders' wagon, scattered the saddle horses standing idly by with a flourish of his hat, and then joined Holly.

Snatching up the reins, he shook them slightly. Getting out of the clearing without attracting the rawhiders' attention was going to be tricky—a move that must be made slow and easy. Shifting the lines to his left hand, he drew his gun as the horses began a slow walk toward the trail, then glanced back.

Cud Hooker suddenly went down when Fargo landed a hard right to his jaw, but it was only for a moment as Cud was up quickly and, both arms swinging, crowded in on Smith. Fargo gave ground before the piston-like driving of Hooker's fists and shortly began to stagger. Both men were plastered with sweat and dust, and blood was showing on both their taut, bewhiskered faces.

Buckman looked ahead. Still a long fifty yards to the trail. He turned his attention to the saddle horses. They had moved off only a short distance instead of trotting off onto the flat as he'd hoped. His luck hadn't been too good there, but so far, where the three rawhiders were concerned, it was still holding. Hooker and Fargo, locked in each other's arms as each struggled to throw the other to the ground, were still oblivious to what had taken place, and Rooster yet lay sprawled where he had fallen.

But even as he watched Matt saw good fortune end. Rooster stirred and sat up, one hand exploring the back of his head gingerly. Suddenly full sensibility returned to him. Twisting about he saw the Gannon wagon with Matt and Holly aboard moving steadily toward the roadway. Scrambling to his feet he rushed forward through the dust pall to Cud and Fargo, yelling and waving his arms.

Delaying no further, Matt put the team of duns into a run, and turning about fired a shot in the direction of the saddle horses. The bullet kicked up dirt directly in front of them. They shied away, separating, and, heads held high in alarm, trotted off—again only for a short distance before halting.

Gunshots broke out in the camp in the next moment as Rooster and Fargo Smith opened up with their pistols. But the Gannon team, now racing along at full speed, had carried the wagon well out of range of the handguns, and the rawhiders' bullets fell short.

That advantage wouldn't hold for long, however, Matt knew. Even a fine team like the span of duns could not outrun men on horseback simply because of the heavy drag and burden the wagon put on them. But if they could reach the dense grove that lay in the distance far enough ahead of the rawhiders there would be a slim chance of eluding them.

The horses galloping hard, Matt settled himself as best he could on the seat. It wasn't comfortable. Gannon, a man of short stature, had apparently lowered the seat in order for the upper part of his legs to be level while he drove. The arrangement had an opposite effect for Matt Buckman; a tall man, his knees were now thrust high and he felt as if he were sitting at an angle.

He looked back through the canvas arch of the wagon. The rawhiders had caught up their horses, both Fargo and Cud Hooker taking to the saddle. Rooster had been assigned to drive the hide-loaded vehicle, no doubt because it would travel slower, and Cud and Fargo had a burning desire to catch up with Matt and Holly Gannon and be the first to lay hands on them.

Holly. . . . Matt had given no time to thoughts of her once he'd gotten the Gannon wagon under way. Now he cast a sidelong look at her. Sitting stiffly upright, one hand grasping the iron rail of the seat, feet firmly braced against the floorboards, she was staring straight ahead. There was no hint of fear on her smooth, tanned features, only a tight-lipped defiance.

"We've got a chance if we can make it to those trees," he said, pointing.

The girl turned to face him. The duns were at full speed now, and the wagon was beginning to sway a bit.

"Why?" she asked in an icy tone.

"Why?" Buckman echoed in surprise. "Means we'll both stay alive. If we don't, if they run us down, we're done for."

"It makes no difference to me," Holly said. "Either way I lose."

Matt threw another look back to the rawhiders. Fargo and Cud were still well back but he knew his team could not hold their lead for much longer.

"You—you're thinking I'm like them—"

It was difficult to talk. The thunder of the horses' hooves, the spiraling dust, the creaking and the popping of the wagon, and the rush of the wind past them made their words all but inaudible.

"You are," Holly said. "You're one of them. I saw you—"

"You saw me drive up with that wagon. I sure didn't take a hand in the holdup and shootings."

"What difference does it make? You're one of the

outlaws, and you're as guilty of murdering my folks as the rest of them."

Matt saw a look of horror pass across the girl's features as the recollection of those moments and what had transpired later flooded through her mind again.

"Not what you think," he said, shaking his head. "I'll tell you about it if we can get rid of them and—"

The wagon yawed wildly and began to slide sideways. Buckman, half rising, slowed the horses as he sought to bring the vehicle under control. Standing, legs spread to brace himself like a chariot driver of old, he finally managed to straighten out the staggering wagon without losing too much time and ground.

But the near-accident had not been without cost. He could see that Hooker and Fargo Smith had gained considerably on them. And on beyond them and their straining horses he caught a glimpse of Rooster Drumm through the dust coming on fast in the rawhiders' wagon with the third saddle horse trailing close by.

The grove was just ahead—no more than a quarter mile. It appeared dark and well studded with trees and brush. It would be no easy task driving the wagon through it, Matt realized, and Hooker and Fargo, on horseback, would have all the advantage.

Once again settled on the uncomfortable seat, Buckman weighed their chances of successfully completing the escape. They were thin at best, but if he could reach the trees, get well into the grove before the rawhiders overtook them, he could perhaps find a place to halt and hide for a few moments, and hope that Hooker and the others would search the wrong area for Holly Gannon and him. But there was small hope of that, too. Like as not it would come down to a shoot-out between him and the three men and the odds for his surviving that weren't good.

They reached the grove with the horses heaving for wind. It was more thinly populated with trees than Matt had thought when viewing it from the distance, but there was considerable tall, dense brush among the cottonwoods and scrub oaks, and here and there weed- and rock-studded mounds broke the flatness.

Grim, Buckman headed the team straight into the shadowy area, the wagon jolting and rocking from side to side when the wheels passed over clumps of low bushes, exposed roots, and grassy hummocks. He could not hear the rawhiders because of the racket the Gannon wagon was setting up, but Matt knew Cud and Fargo could not be far behind.

An arroyo appeared directly in front of the team, turned frantic by the wild passage through the clawing, restraining brush. Instantly Matt swung the wagon down into the wash and began to double back east. On the smooth, sandy floor of the arroyo the vehicle rolled more quietly, and, listening, he could now hear Hooker and Fargo Smith somewhere below as they crashed their way through the grove. Shortly the rattle of the rawhiders' wagon reached him; Rooster had arrived, was also nearby.

"Which way'd he go?"

It was Cud Hooker's voice. The words were faint, barely audible.

"Hell—I don't know! Figured you was keeping him in sight." Fargo Smith's reply was equally indistinct. "Expect he kept on going."

Hope lifted within Matt. His turning into the arroyo and heading back upcountry had fooled the rawhiders; they believed he had continued on down the grove.

"Maybe our chances are getting better," he muttered, and slapping the duns with slack in the lines he urged them to a faster pace.

Holly had made no further comments. She still sat rigidly on the seat, one hand gripping the side rail, the other clenched and resting in her lap. She was not accepting him as a savior and friend, one who had done her a great favor, Matt realized, and that brought a hard, wry grin to his lips. The hell with it, let her think what she wished; he had to help her whether she believed his motive or not; he could not under any circumstances leave her or any other woman there in the brutal hands of Fargo Smith and Cud Hooker.

The arroyo began to narrow. Matt, rising to a half-upright posture again in an effort to see farther, looked ahead as well as to the sides. The wash dwindled into little more than a gully less than a hundred yards on. To the left was the thinning grove, and beyond it he could see the plain where the trail cut its course on westward. To his right were low, ragged hills overgrown with yucca, thistle, false sage, and other rank growth.

The hills were their best bet, Buckman decided.

The grove, which had been their salvation earlier, was mostly behind them now, and no longer as dense; too, turning back into it in the hopes of remaining undiscovered by the rawhiders would be foolish. When Hooker and his partners did not find them below they would immediately turn and work their way back up through the trees and undergrowth, probing every possibility much like soldiers in a forage line.

Buckman gave the problem no further thought and, keeping an eye on the east bank of the arroyo, waited until he located a break in the dark, rocky soil and then wheeled the team and wagon up and out of the wash. It was a rough few moments during which the vehicle pitched and tossed violently, and its contents slammed back and forth against the sides of the bed, but the team did not falter, and soon they were back up on fairly level ground.

Matt, rising again for a better look at the country before them as well as to stretch his cramped legs, saw that they were on the fringe of a rugged, broken area, once much more of a badlands than he had expected. It would be hard going for the horses, but the nature of the country would offer many hiding places for the team and wagon, and with a bit of luck they just might get Hooker and the others off their heels.

Wrapping the lines around the whipstock, Matt reached back into the jumble of Gannon family possessions in the bed of the wagon and, seizing a wool lap robe, dropped to the ground. Hurrying to the point where he had driven the vehicle up out of the arroyo, he swept out all signs of the exit with the robe and further covered over the place with brush. That done he began to work back toward the wagon, sweeping out the imprints of the iron-tired wheels and the horses' hooves as he went until he reached the point where he had halted.

Climbing back into the wagon, Matt tossed the robe into the bed; settling onto the seat, he took up the reins. As he put the horses into motion he glanced at Holly.

"Going to have a rough ride for a bit. Got to get back in these hills where nobody'll spot us."

The girl made no reply, actually gave no indication that she had heard his words, but simply sat in stiff silence, fingers of one hand still locked to the seat rail, the others clenched into a small fist that lay idle in her lap.

Buckman shrugged and centered his attention on driving. Let Holly Gannon think what she wished, he had the task of getting them hidden in the maze of bluffs, gullies, hills, and ragged growth, which was more important than wasting time humoring her.

The wagon moved slow, its wheels at times cutting deep into the loose sand, on other occasions striking solidly against and then rolling over half-buried rocks. The horses began to tire and sweat darkened their hides, but Buckman kept them moving on, winding in and out of the hills and dark-faced bluffs until late in the afternoon they came to a fairly wide arroyo that entered the swale along which they were traveling, at right angles.

Without hesitation Matt turned into it. If it developed that Hooker and the others were not fooled by his covering tactics back at the wash and followed them into the hills, he would be in a position to see their approach far enough in advance to be ready for them.

Glancing up at the steel-blue sky and the sun, now well to the west, Matt again secured the lines to the handle of the socketed whip, and turned to the girl.

"Can climb down now if you want. We'll be spending the night here."

Holly stubbornly continued to stare out across the broken land. Buckman waited out a brief minute for a response, and when none came he shook his head, realization of the fear the girl was experiencing coming to him.

"No sense being scared of me," he said gently. "I ain't about to hurt you."

"You expect me to believe that?" she demanded angrily, suddenly facing him. "You're one of them; you can't deny it! A thief and a killer—and you and those other men murdered my mother and father—and now you've kidnapped me!"

Matt stirred impatiently. "Would you have liked it better if I'd left you back there for Fargo and Hooker to fight over and claim?"

"I can't see as I'm much better off," she replied, a bit more calm. "You probably have the same thing planned for me that they did."

Matt swore softly. "I wasn't one of them. Sure wish I could make you see—"

"You were with them—helped them do what they did—"

"Only because I found myself in a jackpot and had to throw in with them."

Moisture dampened Holly's cheeks and upper lip but there was no diminishing of the hate that filled her eyes.

"Hard to believe you didn't have a choice!" she said icily.

"I sure as hell didn't," Buckman snapped, patience wearing thin. "Renegade Indians had me pinned down. They would have finished me off if Hooker and the others hadn't come along and bailed me out."

"You could have gone on your way after that. You didn't have to stay with them," Holly pointed out in the same disbelieving tone.

"Indians got my horse and gear; everything I owned, in fact, except what was on my back. Was no way I could go on." Buckman paused, brushed at the sweat on his forehead. "Lady, I would've liked to kept going; I sure wasn't happy over lining up with a bunch of rawhiders—or what I figured were rawhiders."

"Rawhiders? What's that mean?"

"Hide hunters—people who go about the country skinning out dead horses and cattle—buffalo, too, if they find any—and then sell the hides. With Hooker and the others that's only a cover. They make their money robbing and killing.

"Soon as I knew that I tried to figure a way I could pull out, but I couldn't come up with anything. There was a U.S. marshal come along and I looked for a chance to tell him what Cud and the others were, but I had to give that up. If I'd tried I would've got him killed. Fargo was holding a gun on him all the time he was there."

"I don't see why you couldn't have taken one of their horses, stolen it, and ridden out. That you didn't proves to me that you didn't want to—that you're just like they are."

"I explained how—"

"Nothing you've said has been the truth; I know that. And you can't tell me—"

"Looks like I'm not going to be able to tell you anything," Matt broke in, voice filled with disgust. "But I'll say this so's you'll know: Hooker and the others didn't trust me much and kept a close eye on everything I did. If I'd tried to steal a horse and make a run for it I would've got a bullet in my back before I'd gone fifty feet."

Turning about, Buckman put a foot on the wheel and dropped to the ground. Pausing, he looked back up at Holly.

"Now, you go right ahead and think what you like. Makes not one whit of difference to me." He started to move off, hesitated again. Reaching into a pocket of his vest he obtained the wedding ring he had removed from Mattie Gannon's finger.

"Figured you might like to have this for a keepsake," he said, handing it to her, and then walked on.

16

Circling to the rear of the wagon Matt stared at the confusion of household items, clothing, minor articles of furniture, and other family possessions. Somewhere among the mess there should be a sack of grain, possibly even a pair of nose bags for the duns. Gannon had started the journey west well prepared, and with such a fine team he undoubtedly would be thinking of their care and needs.

Climbing up into the vehicle Buckman began to dig around in the disorder and shortly came up with a full sack of oats. Evidently Caleb Gannon had replenished his supply at the last settlement stop. There were no nose bags to be found, but there were two gallon-size buckets apparently used for feeding and watering. Filling each half-full of the grain, Matt carried them to the gray-brown geldings, set them on the ground in front of them, pulled slack in the lines, and let the duns eat.

He should remove the bridles, he knew, but with the possibility of having to move out on a moment's notice a reality, he was reluctant to do anything that would impede an immediate flight should the rawhiders show up.

Holly was still sitting on the seat, stiff and unyielding, her face tipped down, eyes on the bit of gold jewelry he had salvaged and given her. She looked up as he halted at the front wheel.

"This ring—it was mean—a cruel thing to do," she said brokenly. "Giving it to me only reminds me of what happened, of what you did."

Buckman's features tightened as he stared at her. After a bit he shrugged in frustration. "Best we straighten up things in the wagon. Have to make a bed—"

"I'll not stay in here with you!" Holly all but screamed the words. "You can't make—"

"I won't be anywheres close," Buckman said quietly, "so rest easy. Wagon's all yours."

One of the geldings had overturned his feed bucket. It was making no difference to him as he continued to snuff up the grain hungrily. He'd water them in an hour or so, Matt reminded himself; they'd had a hard day and this was their first feed and water.

Continuing on to the rear of the wagon, Buckman drew himself aboard and, starting in the area directly behind the seat, began to separate and reorganize the load into some semblance of order, uncovering almost at once the rifle Caleb Gannon had dropped after being shot. Jacking a fresh cartridge into the chamber, Matt hooked a thumb over the curved hammer and lowered it into the safety position. Standing the weapon in the corner of the wagon bed, he glanced up, saw Holly watching him, a sort of revulsion blanking her features.

"May need that gun," he said. "Want it to be handy and ready."

Holly's lips compressed. "I—I hate guns—the killing that goes with them."

Matt frowned. "Haven't you ever fired one?"

"No—never! I won't touch a weapon of any kind!"

"Better change your mind about that right now," Buckman said brusquely. "Time may come when it'll mean the difference in living or dying."

Matt supposed he should expect that attitude from her: an Easterner who probably never faced danger of any sort greater than not being asked to dance at the weekly schoolhouse frolic. But for her own good, and probably his, she should become familiar with weapons.

"Be a good thing if you'll learn how to shoot, specially a rifle," Matt said resignedly, taking up the weapon. "You only have to pull the hammer back, aim—that means point the gun—at whatever you want to hit, and then sort of press real easy on the trigger. Works the same with a six-shooter."

Holly, watching indifferently, showed little interest. "I doubt the time will ever come when I'll want to use a gun of any kind."

"Wrong there. Out in this part of the country you need to know how. Don't like saying this, but if you had known how you could've helped your pa some and maybe he and your ma would be alive right now. . . . Now, coming back to rifle, once you shoot you need a fresh cartridge. All you have to do is work this lever. It throws out the spent one and slides a new one into the chamber. After you've done that you're ready to shoot again."

Holly started to turn away, paused as Matt stood

the rifle once again in the corner of the wagon bed. "My folks, were they—did you bury them properly?"

Matt nodded. "Rooster and me together took care of it. Did the best we could."

"But you didn't have a coffin. How—"

"Took a quilt and wrapped them in it. After the grave was covered over I piled rocks on top of the grave to keep the varmints from digging into it."

Holly shuddered. Sometime during the time when she was being held captive one sleeve of her checked shirt had ripped loose at the shoulder, and a smear of grease, probably from the hub of the wagon wheel to which she had been tied, stained the front of her shirt.

"It's all so unreal, so hard to believe," she murmured, eyes now on a pair of camp robber jays contesting one of the horses for the grain spilled on the ground. "This country—it's so savage, so terribly uncivilized—it and the people in it! It's hard to think it's a part of the United States. And it's ugly—and empty."

"You get used to that," Buckman said, settling back his hands on the grub box—one of the items he'd been searching for. "And you'll come to think it's a real pretty land one day—"

"I doubt that," Holly snapped. "No, I never will!"

Matt, the box of foodstuff and cooking utensils in his hands, worked his way to the rear of the wagon and jumped to the ground.

"I've got the grub. Won't be able to make a fire and do any cooking tonight, but I expect we can find something in the box we can eat. You best finish straightening out that mess in the wagon where you'll be sleeping. I've got something else to do."

"What's that?" Holly demanded suspiciously.

"Aim to back track our trail for a ways and see if there's any sign of those rawhiders moving in on us." Stepping up to the wagon, he reached in and obtained the rifle. "Might need this," he said, and then added, "I won't be gone long."

Saying no more Buckman moved off, staying close to the brush as much as possible as he retraced their course through the hills. After he'd covered a mile and spent a good half hour on a high knoll studying the country between him and the grove, and seeing no sign of life other than a coyote making a meal of a rabbit, he started back for the camp.

Evidently Hooker and his partners had failed to find the tracks of Gannon's wagon and were still hunting through the brush-and-tree area for the girl and him. And with darkness now only a short time away they likely would give up the search until morning. At least, Matt hoped it would be that way, but he knew he could take nothing for granted; it would be necessary that he keep watch on the trail throughout the night.

At the wagon he found Holly still going about the task of rearranging the contents of the vehicle and preparing a bed for herself. Standing the rifle against a nearby rock where it would be available, Matt moved on to the horses, and taking up the buckets filled them with water from the keg lashed to a shelf on the side of the vehicle. The team's thirst satisfied, Buckman put the tin containers back inside the wagon and turned to the grub box.

Holly, now standing off to one side, the chore of rearranging the vehicle's contents completed, watched him closely. In deference to the bright, slanting sunshine she had added a small, white straw hat to what she was wearing. In spite of the hostility between them it brought a half smile to Matt Buckman's lips. Holly Gannon was a mighty fetching girl despite her torn and grease-smudged dress.

"What will we do tomorrow?" she asked as he opened the box and began to go through it in quest of something with which to make a meal.

"Try to stay clear of Cud Hooker and his friends," he replied, producing a jar of some kind of preserves and a lone hard biscuit. "You mind coming over here and seeing what you can find in here that won't need cooking? You know more about what's in this box than I do."

Holly moved forward hesitantly, stopped after a step or two. Buckman's jaw hardened. He swore softly. The girl was afraid of him, still considered him on the same level as Fargo Smith, Hooker, and Rooster Drumm. Anger flamed through him suddenly.

"What's eating you?" he snarled. "I ain't going to hurt you," he added, rising and backing away.

"I don't trust you," Holly stated flatly. "And I don't want to have anything to do with you. Far as I'm concerned you're no better than your partners—"

"Not partners of mine! I've told you that—"

"Yes, you've told me, but that doesn't say it's true. And if it's my father's money you're leading up to asking me about—maybe even forcing me to talk and tell where it is—I don't know. I've never seen it."

Matt's mouth pulled into a hard grin. "Not that it matters a damn, but I don't think he brought any big sack of cash along with him. Hooker and Fargo tore that wagon apart and never found it—and it wasn't on him."

Holly shivered, evidently having a momentary recollection of Hooker's insistent hands probing her body. "He had several thousand dollars. I guess he must have had the bank forward it to where we were going—Wickenburg, in Arizona."

"Well, I'm not interested in it—or you," Buckman said, still angry. "Only in your team and wagon."

"I won't believe anything you say," the girl declared stubbornly. She had come over to the grub box, was crouched beside it going through its contents. "You're one of them, and, like I've said, I won't trust you."

"And I'm not hashing over what I've told you about Hooker and his bunch, and me again, either," Buckman said angrily. "It's the truth whether you want to believe it or not."

"I choose not to," Holly said coolly. "Here's some slices of dried beef and a wedge of cheese, and some other things. You can make your supper on them."

Matt came forward and picked up several slices of the meat, and the cheese the girl had placed alongside several biscuits on the lid of the box. As he approached she rose and backed to the wagon.

"You're not eating anything?" he asked, again impatient.

Holly shook her head. "I'm not hungry," she said, and climbing up into the wagon dropped the canvas curtains at both the rear and the front of the vehicle.

Matt stood silently by, waiting until she had become quiet; then, taking the food and tucking the rifle under an arm, he crossed to a high point at the intersection of the swale and the arroyo, where he had a long view of the trail, and settled down. He was tired, hungry, in need of sleep, and all out of sorts—thanks to the flourishing animosity existing between Holly and him. But there was nothing he could do about most of it. He'd have to stay awake: Hooker, Fargo Smith, and Rooster Drumm just might find the tracks of the Gannon team and wagon and try to move in.

Alone in the hot semidarkness of the wagon, Holly curled up on her pallet and wept bitterly. She was so alone—so utterly alone—in a world of death and violence, and in the hands of a killer, one of those who had taken the lives of her parents.

She didn't know what to expect next. Matt, as he was called, had expressed no plans for her other than to say they must keep clear of his three partners—all evil-smelling horrible men who thought nothing of committing murder, and worse where she was concerned.

Fortunately for her, Matt did seem the best of the lot, but that really had no bearing on anything. That he was cleaner and lacked the terrible odor that emanated from the others was no recommendation. He was one of them regardless of his protests to the contrary; the fact that there were three saddle horses and a wagon matched exactly the number of men necessary to ride and drive was proof of such.

It had been greed, not a desire to help her, that prompted Matt to seize the opportunity back at the Gannon camp, and make an escape. When two of the outlaws had become engaged in a brawl, he had jumped at the chance, knocking out the third rawhider with a blow to the head and then fleeing with her in her father's wagon. Matt's motive was not difficult to understand; he simply wanted her for himself rather than allowing the one called Fargo to claim her, as well as taking possession of the team, the wagon, and what he hoped to find, her father's money.

She had tried to explain that she knew nothing about the money, that if her father had brought any large amount along she was unaware of the fact. Like as not he'd had the banker in Carlisle forward a draft to Wickenburg, but she had no way of knowing that for certain, either.

And likely she never would know what had become of the money. It was lost—lost somewhere, somehow. One would think her father, being the good businessman that he was, would have taken her into his confidence, but he had said nothing.

Sitting up, Holly brushed at the tears on her cheeks and dabbed at her eyes. It had occurred to her that weeping and self-pity was gaining nothing for her. Too, she could expect no help from anyone for the plain and simple reason that she didn't know anyone in this bleak, godforsaken land. A frown tugged at her brow; there was the doctor and the storekeeper back in Edom.

At once hope lifted within Holly. If she could manage to get back to the settlement she would at least be among decent, honorable people. And there she could likely persuade someone to drive her back to Pennsylvania with the promise that she'd pay them in full by selling off the team and wagon once there. Too, in Edom she could tell the constable about the rawhiders; he could then get some men together, hunt down the outlaws, and put an end to the robbing and killing that was taking place along the trail.

Getting back to Edom was the problem, Holly realized. She hadn't the faintest idea where it lay or how to find it. Somewhere to the east—that was logical—but buried in a bewilderment of look-alike hills and bluffs as she presently was, getting there could become next to an impossibility for her.

The answer to the problem came to her suddenly. There was a way, and Matt—who had shown her how to use a gun—would provide it.

17

The night was bright and cool. Stars littered the sky and moonlight flooded the land with a soft, silvery glow. Coyotes wailed from a half dozen distant points, and the hooting of an owl off in the grove to the west seemed only paces away while the rustling of mice in the grass and weeds around him was a constant sound. Matt did not mind; the distractions helped him stay awake, for despite all efforts he dozed occasionally.

Morning came in a blaze of glorious color, and rousing himself Matt moved back to the wagon. He was hungry and guessed that Holly Gannon no doubt was also in need of a good meal, as she had passed up any food the evening before. He was reluctant to build a fire as there was no way of knowing where the rawhiders were at that moment, but he felt it was a risk he'd have to take. The answer was to prepare a meal quickly and get it over with fast, then be on their way west.

Buckman began to search about for aged, dry wood that would create a minimum of smoke. It took some time, as growth in the hills was scant, but he finally accumulated what he considered a sufficient amount, and raking together a horseshoe of small stones to form a firebox he got a fire going, set the coffeepot, which he filled from the keg, over the flames, and then turned to prepare a meal.

Gannon had just recently replenished his stock of grub, Matt saw, probably at some town back up the trail, and it was no chore to get together a breakfast of ham, potatoes, heated biscuits to be spread with honey, and of course black coffee in short time. He was just finishing up frying the potatoes when he heard Holly leave the wagon and step in behind him.

"It'll help if you'll dig out a couple of cups and plates, and something to eat with," he said without looking around. "Grub's just about ready."

In the next moment a sharp blow to the head stunned Buckman, sent him rocking forward. Reacting, he threw himself to one side to keep from falling across the fire and the food he was preparing. In those same moments he felt Holly jerk his pistol from its holster. Seething with anger, he rolled away and faced her.

"What the hell do you—" he began and stopped short.

The girl, holding the .45 with both trembling hands, the hammer drawn back to full cock position, was aiming the weapon directly at him. Moving slowly and carefully he sat up. The gun had a hair trigger. Holly had only to apply the slightest pressure and the gun would fire.

"For crissake, lady—be careful," he said hoarsely. "That gun will go off easy." The possibility of such was doubled by the fact that she was unfamiliar with the pistol—with any gun, he'd learned earlier.

Holly, lips tight, body tense, eyes filled with determination, shook her head. "It won't go off if you do what I tell you," she said, "but if you try anything —I'll use it."

A wry grin pulled at Buckman's mouth. "Don't worry, I ain't about to," he said, and then swore harshly as the girl took the rifle he'd leaned against a clump of brush by the barrel and threw it off as far as she could into the arroyo.

"We just might need that," he said.

"One gun will be enough—and I'll hang on to it," she replied coolly.

Matt shrugged. "You best hand that gun back to me—"

"No, I've told you before I don't trust you, or believe anything you've said. You're no different from the others, you're one of them, and I can't—"

Matt swore again. "If I was one of them would I be running and hiding to get away?"

"I don't know what you'd do but I suspect all this is just some kind of trick so's you can have everything your way. You've run out on them hoping to get my father's money—make me tell, and then—"

The coffeepot boiled over in a sizzle of liquid spilling onto the flames. Matt, again careful, reached out slowly and, wincing when his fingers touched the handle, set it off the fire. Taking advantage of the moment, he removed the frying pan as well.

"You're wrong about that," he said.

Matt was hoping Holly had lowered the gun but when he turned his attention back to her she was still standing as she had been—half crouched, hands tightly gripping the heavy weapon, finger on the trigger, hammer cocked. He had thought his brief instructions to her earlier on how to use both a rifle and a six-gun had fallen on uninterested ears, but he had guessed wrong. The girl had grasped the rudiments, if nothing else.

"You're driving me to the nearest town," Holly said. "I can handle the team, but with outlaws like you and your friends hiding behind every bush and rock, I'd never make it alone."

"Just what I aimed to do," Matt said. "Just as soon as we could get out of here."

Holly considered him skeptically. "I doubt that. First chance you got you would—"

"I ain't about to even take a deep breath long as you're standing there holding that gun on me," Matt cut in angrily. "Hand it back and we'll talk things out."

"There's no talking to be done," Holly said in a resolute tone. "I've told you what you're going to do: drive me back up the trail to Edom, that's a town east of here, where I can hire somebody to go the rest of the way home with me."

Matt was shaking his head even before she had finished speaking. "We'd be a fool to go that way. Not only be taking a chance of running into those renegade Kiowas again but we'd be sure to meet up with Hooker and his bunch—"

"I don't believe there ever were any renegade Indians," Holly said. "We didn't see any along the trail. I think you just made that up—a lie."

"You were lucky," Buckman said. "Now, I'm willing to drive you to where you can sell your outfit and catch a stage, or hire on a driver if that's what you want—but it will be to Santa Fe, on west of here."

"It's Edom that I want to go to," Holly said stubbornly, "and you'll take me there."

"Only way I'll do that is if you're holding that gun on me—and you'd have to do it every minute of the day and night."

"I can, and I will if I have to—"

Matt shrugged wearily. "All right, but we sure won't be doing nothing if we don't eat and get out of here. Hooker and the others are probably around somewheres, maybe close, and they could smell our fire. . . . If you don't figure to shoot me dead right now with that gun would you mind pointing some other way? It's making me mighty nervous."

Holly stirred. Some of the tenseness left her rigid body, and backing up a few steps she circled to the opposite side of the fire. Sitting down on a rock she laid the still-cocked .45 on the ground beside her.

"I'll keep it," she stated. Then, "Plates and cups are in the box, along with forks and such. You can put some of that ham and potatoes and a biscuit on a plate for me. I'll have some of the coffee later."

"Best you drink it while you're eating," Matt said, dragging the grub box in closer to him. "We won't have time for later."

Holly said nothing, and a few moments later warily accepted the food and a cup of the steaming black brew.

"Nothing in that box to eat with," Matt said when she looked inquiringly at him.

Holly nodded. "There's another box in the wagon. The forks and such are probably in it along with some more groceries. Never mind getting it," she added as Buckman started to rise. "I can eat with my fingers."

Matt, breathing easier now that he was no longer looking into the muzzle of his own .45, filled his plate and cup and began to eat. The need to move on as soon as possible was pushing at him relentlessly, and while he didn't know exactly how matters were going to work out, considering Holly Gannon's stubborn attitude, he did know they were in constant danger from the rawhiders as long as they were in the general area of the grove.

Buckman, cleaning off his plate, helped himself to a second cup of coffee. As he took a swallow he glanced across at Holly. She was about finished with what was on her plate, too, either finally realizing the danger of staying there too long or being hungry, Matt was not sure which.

Downing the last of his still-hot coffee Buckman rose, began to collect the cooking gear and stow it away in the box. Taking up the coffeepot he looked at the girl. She shook her head, indicating she wanted no more. Dumping the contents onto the fire, Matt added the pot to the other utensils in the grub box and walked to the horses. They appeared well rested despite having spent the night hitched to the wagon, and while it might have been wise to take time and feed them again he reckoned they could get by until later in the day.

Checking the harness and finding everything satisfactory, Matt retraced his steps to where Holly was waiting. In his absence she had put the remaining dishes and cups in the box and now, pistol in hand again, was standing off to the side.

"Put the box in the wagon," she directed. "Then we can move out—east."

Buckman picked up the wooden container and carried it to the rear of the vehicle, where he placed it inside. Coming about he faced the girl.

"We can't go east—better get that straight."

"I think we can; you just don't want to. Why, I'm not sure."

"I've told you. Too risky. Good chance of running into those renegade Kiowa Indians—and into Hooker and his bunch."

"I doubt our chances are any worse going that way than they would be if we do what you want—"

Matt swore, pulled off his hat, and ran fingers through his hair in exasperation. "Can't tell you nothing, can I?" he said.

A half smile broke the tightness of Holly's features. "No, you can't. Now get up on the seat," she ordered, keeping the pistol leveled at him as she slowly circled the wagon.

Buckman made his way to a front wheel, stepped on the hub, and swung up onto the seat. Taking up the lines he glanced at the girl. This could be his chance to take his gun away from her. He'd watch for an opportunity when she was engaged in climbing up to a place beside him.

But Holly Gannon was apparently aware of that possibility, too. "Turn your back; keep looking the other way," she directed.

Buckman did as directed while, keeping the

cocked weapon trained on him, the girl drew herself up into the wagon and onto the seat beside him.

"It all right to move out now?" he asked, voice heavy with sarcasm.

Holly nodded, and as he clucked the team into and began to cut the rig about, she slipped over the seat into the back of the wagon.

"I'll ride back here," Holly said. "That way you won't get any ideas."

As she spoke Matt felt the muzzle of the pistol against his spine. Angry, he pulled the team to a halt.

"We ain't going nowhere until you take that gun out of my back," he said flatly.

Holly quickly withdrew the .45. "All right, but you remember that I'm sitting here with it aimed at you. If you try anything—like taking me to somewhere other than Edom—I'll shoot you! And don't think I don't know which direction is east."

"You're loco, plain loco," Buckman said in disgust as he put the dun geldings into motion again. "And if you don't know what that word means back where you came from, it means crazy."

"I'd be a lunatic to trust you!" Holly shot back. "You haven't fooled me one bit acting like you're my friend and wanting to help and all that. You're one of those rawhiders, as you call them, and you— you kidnapped me just so you wouldn't have to share anything with them."

Matt was only half listening as he drove the team back over the winding route that had brought them into the desolate area where they had made camp. He wanted to avoid the grove—odds were that

Hooker and his partners were still somewhere within it—but it would first be necessary to get out of the endless hill country that extended indefinitely on, like varying tan and brown bubbles, to the east and south.

"I don't know where Papa's money is, so—"

"Can quit harping on that damn money!" Buckman snapped. "Told you I'm not interested in it."

Holly sighed as the wagon rocked and jolted over the rough terrain. "I guess I am—more than I've let on. He had several thousand dollars from the sale of the hardware store back home. It means the difference of a future or no future at all for me."

"Hate to see you lose it," Matt said, his tone softening. "Good chance he did have it sent on ahead, but pilgrims don't usually do that. Seem to want to carry all their cash with them."

"That's the way Papa would have done it, I'm sure. He was never one to trust banks much, and he kept his money and important papers in a safe at home. Makes me think he'd hardly do business with some banker he didn't know in a far-off town that he'd never been to."

"Can promise you this," Buckman said, shifting so that his cramped legs could straighten out, "it sure wasn't on him or anywhere in this wagon. Hooker and Fargo are mighty good when it comes to looking for something. They would have found it for sure."

"Could one of them discovered it, tucked it inside his shirt or something to hide it from the other?"

Matt's shoulders stirred. He glanced over his shoulder at Holly. She was sitting on the floor of the wagon bed, gun still cocked and aimed at him. The sight sent a chill through him. The hair-triggered weapon in her inexperienced hands was a real threat. If the wagon rocked too sharply, or veered suddenly, the .45 could discharge—and he'd be a dead man.

"Want you to point that gun some other way," he said. "Hair on the back of my neck's standing up like quills on a porcupine—"

"What about what I said?" the girl insisted, lowering the weapon slightly. "Could that be what happened?"

"Maybe," Matt said, feeling some relieved, "but I don't see how either one of them could've got away with it. Whatever—if one of them did, the money's sure gone for good now."

Holly made no comment but a quiet sound coming from her caused him to again glance over his shoulder at her. She was weeping softly, her eyes on the gold wedding ring of her mother's that she was wearing on a finger of her right hand.

"Yes, it's lost—for certain—just like everything else," she said in a hopeless voice. "All I can do is make the best of what's left."

"Selling off this rig will give you a start. That team of duns is worth quite a bit of money. So's the wagon. With what you'll get for the outfit you'll be able to buy a ticket back to your home in Pennsylvania, and maybe have enough left over to live on for a while."

"Maybe," Holly said, wiping at her eyes with the back of her free hand. Straightening up she looked past Matt at the country visible to her. "Shouldn't we be turning east?"

"Back in your home town," Buckman said, ignoring the question and hopeful of keeping her thoughts on something other than the direction she was insisting they take, "don't you have a relative, or maybe a close friend of the family who'll give you a hand?"

They had broken out of the hills and were once again in open country. All that was left now to do was cross through the grove, which lay just ahead beyond the arroyo they had followed earlier when escaping from the rawhiders, and reach the east-west trail.

That was when the final decision as to whether they would do as Holly wished—double back to Edom—or take what he was certain was the safer route on west to Santa Fe would have to be made. And to do that Matt Buckman knew it would be necessary to recover his gun, to physically take it away from the girl. Only then would he have a chance to make her see reason.

"There's no one that's close," Holly replied. "I suppose—"

She broke off suddenly. Buckman had abruptly come upright on the seat. Off to their left a hundred yards or so in the grove he had seen motion.

"What is it? What's the matter?" Holly asked anxiously.

Buckman swore tautly. "It's Hooker and the others," he said in a grim voice as the wagon, led by Fargo and Rooster Drumm, came into full view.

18

"What can we do?" Holly asked, fear lifting her voice.

Matt jerked the whip out of its holder. "Get out of here—fast," he said, and then added: "Watch that damn gun! I don't want it going off when we hit a bump and blowing me to kingdom come!"

He didn't look back to see if the girl had laid the pistol aside but put his mind on moving out and getting as much of a lead on the rawhiders as possible before they spotted him and the Gannon wagon. The best course to follow was once again in the grove. While the underbrush and trees did slow the speed of the wagon somewhat, they also afforded a degree of protection and cover.

A yell went up from one of the rawhiders. Fargo's voice, Matt thought. Plying the whip, he sent the horses racing around the upper end of the arroyo, across a narrow flat for the grove. As he reached the fringe of the growth he threw a glance in the direction of the outlaws. They had gotten under way quickly, were now coming on—Fargo and Rooster Drumm well out in front of the wagon being driven by Cud Hooker.

A shot rang out, echoed flatly. Matt risked another look at the rawhiders. It had been Rooster who had fired. His arm was still up with the pistol in hand. Abruptly he glanced toward Hooker, and then holstered his weapon. Evidently Cud had ordered him not to shoot, believing no doubt they could easily run down the Gannon wagon, and he didn't want to risk Holly getting shot.

"Are we going to get away?" Matt heard the girl ask in a voice muffled by the noise of the vehicle.

"Sure aim to try," he replied, looking back at her. She was still holding his .45, he noted, but the weapon was no longer pointed at him. He heaved a sigh of relief. That was one worry off his mind. With the wagon bouncing and jolting from side to side in its reckless flight, the weapon, with its finely honed trigger spring, could have easily gone off.

Buckman turned again to the rawhiders. He could not see Rooster at first, and then he located the man. His horse had apparently stumbled, tripping on an exposed root or some other obstacle. The delay, brief as it was, had allowed Hooker and the wagon to draw abreast, and as Rooster was pulling himself back into the saddle Cud yelled something at the younger man to which Drumm made no reply.

The danger was Fargo Smith. He had raced in close, was now only a few strides behind as they rushed in and out of the trees and brush of the grove. A clearing loomed ahead. Matt swerved, hoping to skirt the bit of open ground. Fargo, seizing the opportunity, cut across it and rode in close to the off dun gelding. Leaning well over he reached for the horse's bridle. Matt shouted to the girl.

"He's going to pull the team down! Shoot him!"

There was no response from Holly. Buckman

twisted half about, and gambling on the team not overturning the wagon, faced the girl.

"Use that gun—shoot!" he yelled above the clatter.

Holly shook her head. "I—I can't! I can't shoot—kill anything—not a man—"

Reaching back Matt grabbed the gun by its barrel, and keeping the muzzle pointed away drew himself back onto the seat. The team was beginning to slow as Fargo dragged at the off dun's headstall. Without taking time to aim Matt triggered the already cocked weapon at the rawhider. Fargo, releasing his grip on the dun's bridle, buckled forward and, as his mount swung away, slid from the saddle and fell to the ground.

Getting Fargo Smith out of it would help but little, Matt realized as the team, again at full speed considering the obstructions in the grove, hurried on. Rooster Drumm was still very much in the chase, and in all likelihood Hooker would forsake the wagon and mount Fargo's horse.

He couldn't expect to outrun the two men, but the odds had improved, and if he could find a good place to stop and make a stand he could probably hold off Hooker and Rooster Drumm until someone might hear the gunshots and take it upon himself to investigate. That could take hours, however, and he wasn't too well fixed for ammunition. The box of extra cartridges he always carried had been lost when the renegade Kiowas got his horse and gear.

The left front wheel of the vehicle struck something large and solid—a rock or the stump of a dead tree. The wagon leaped into the air, twisted about, and came down hard on the opposite wheel as the rear end jackknifed. For a long, harrowing moment it hung there as if undecided whether to right itself or capsize. And then the team, straining in their harness, yanked it back onto all four iron-tired wheels and plunged on.

Matt glanced hurriedly back into the jumble and disorder of the wagon bed. Holly lay sprawled near its center, a dazed look in her eyes. The wild slewing about of the vehicle had apparently hurled her against the solid wood of a side and stunned her. He could see no sign of blood and reckoned she was not seriously hurt.

Yells not far behind drew his attention. The near-accident had cost them time. Their lead on Rooster and on Cud Hooker—now riding Fargo Smith's horse as anticipated—had been cut considerably. Buckman's jaw tightened. The time when he'd have to stop and make a stand was drawing closer with each passing minute. But he'd have to find a place outside the grove. Among the trees and brush clumps it would be too difficult to hold off the two outlaws.

Hooker and Rooster were both near enough now to put bullets into the team, but they were holding back on that, too. Evidently Holly Gannon wasn't all the rawhider wanted unharmed when he finally brought the wagon to a halt; he had his eyes on the team of duns also. Now Hooker was simply biding his time, believing the Gannon wagon would over-turn as it had come near doing a short time before, or the team would tire, slow down, or perhaps even come to a stop.

The brush and trees were thinning. Through the tangle of leaves and branches Matt could see open country. He'd be no better off out there for the team was bound to be tiring and would never be able to stay ahead of the men on horseback. But there were hills in the not too far distance. Maybe, if he could reach them before Hooker and Drumm, he could pull up and find a place to make a stand.

Holly. . . . He risked a glance at her. She had recovered her senses, was sitting up. A darkness was showing along her left temple, an indication of the hard blow she had sustained.

"You all right?" Buckman had to shout in order to be heard above the noise of the wagon and the pound of the horses' hooves.

Holly shrugged, nodded, and tried to see beyond him. "Are they still out there?"

"Following us," he replied and, as the girl turned to look out the rear of the vehicle, added: "We've got to make it to those hills on ahead. It's a cinch we can't outrun them."

At that moment they reached the edge of the grove, burst into the open and onto a flat. The hills, actually an area of ragged mounds and low bluffs littered with black lava rock and overgrown by cactus, weeds, bayonet yucca and the like, were much closer than Matt had thought. Leaning forward he popped the whip over the hard-running team. The duns lowered their heads and responded, the wagon lurching forward slightly as they threw themselves into the harness.

Buckman was wishing he had Gannon's rifle and cartridges to go with it—but the long gun was out.

He'd have to depend entirely on his .45, and that meant wasting no ammunition. Matt looked back. Hooker and Rooster Drumm were now out of the grove and on the flat. They were coming on at an easy gallop, not pushing their horses, he saw. No doubt Cud was doing as suspected: he would simply let the Gannon team run itself out, and then close in.

The lava hills were just ahead, the black volcanic rocks shining dully in the strong sunlight. *Malpaís,* the Spanish and Mexican people called it—bad country—which was an accurate description of it. The sharp-edged rocks could cut a man's boots to shreds should he be forced to walk any distance across them, and all too many horses died from broken legs when they stumbled and fell, thanks to the treacherous footing.

But it all looked good to Matt Buckman. They were going to make it. He could pull up and make a stand feeling that he'd have at least a near-even chance in shooting it out with Cud and Rooster— and maybe come through it alive.

They reached the first of the numerous mounds with the lathered horses heaving for wind. Matt cut in behind it and brought the rig to a stop. There was no point in going further into the lava bed—the first mound looked to be little different from the others. Dropping the lines, he leaped to the ground and spun to assist Holly.

The girl had already crawled over the seat. He held out his arms to her. "Jump!"

Immediately she threw herself from the wagon into his waiting hands, glancing over a shoulder at

Hooker and Drumm now less than fifty yards away, as she did.

"Got to hurry!" Matt yelled and, holding on to Holly's hand, started for the mound. Midway he slowed, altered direction. The hill a few yards off to the left offered better possibilities; there were several large rocks on it and it was covered with taller brush as well.

"This way!" he said tightly, and, all but dragging Holly Gannon behind him, ran for the better choice.

19

They reached the ragged formation of lava and sun-bleached earth, hurried in among the scatter of black rocks, mementos of some gigantic volcanic upheaval in centuries past, and crouched low. Tall weeds surrounded them, and a number of the larger rocks formed a bulwark which afforded protection in the front, but there was little else of consequence to the sides and rear that would effectively shield them. Conditions for making a last-ditch stand were far from ideal; however, it was better than being caught on the open mesa or in the grove.

"Where are they?" Holly asked, leaning against one of the rocks. They were both breathing hard from the short, fast run, and sweat glistened on their faces.

Matt raised his head slightly in order to see beyond the mound. Hooker and Rooster Drumm had halted some forty or fifty yards away and were apparently discussing the situation.

"Sitting out there jawing," Buckman replied, drawing his gun and checking it for loads. "Expect they're trying to figure out the best way to get us out of the *malpaís.*"

Holly repeated the word and listened as Matt explained its meaning. "Lot of volcanoes in this country—one pretty good-sized one north of here. All this probably came from it. They're moving in closer," he added as the rawhiders, still in the saddle, started forward slowly.

Abruptly they were lost to view behind the hill that Matt had picked at first but bypassed when the one they now occupied looked to be larger and to offer greater concealment.

"What—what are they doing now?" Holly asked. Her voice was unsteady and reflected the fear that gripped her.

"Can't see them; they're in behind some rocks. My guess is Hooker's going to let us sit and sweat it out for a bit, and then try coming in on us from two sides."

"Can we—can you stop them?"

"Sure aim to try. Would help plenty if we had another gun—that rifle of your pa's specially."

"I'm sorry I threw it away—but I'm afraid I couldn't use it—not on a man."

"You held my .45 on me—"

"I know, but I wouldn't have shot it. I never could, no matter what. I just wanted to make you do things my way."

Matt brushed at his forehead with the back of a wrist. Heat was mounting steadily among the lava rocks, and by noon—still hours away—it would become unbearable. Would Hooker wait that long? Matt doubted it. The two rawhiders would be finding the heat intense along the side of the mound where they had halted also, and while the temperature would not be near as fierce there as in among the black rocks, it would be very disagreeable. But there was little sense in trying to guess what Cud Hooker would do, Buckman thought; his one choice was to wait and be ready.

The burning minutes wore on. Insects clacked loudly in the weeds, lizards darted across the smaller rocks, and off to the side a rattlesnake, seeking a cooler retreat before the heat reached its peak, slithered in under a brush-shaded ledge. Holly shivered as she watched the diamondback, her eyes filled with horror and revulsion.

"I'll—I'll never get used to this terrible land!" she said in a trembling voice. "Everything is so wild, so threatening—and killing comes so easy."

"Maybe," Matt said, "but you've had the hard luck of seeing only the worst of it. Time will come—if you'd stick around—when you'll see what fine country it is. Mighty pretty, too."

"I'll never stay," Holly declared. "Never! I can't get back to civilization soon enough—if I ever do," she finished, a hopeless strain in her tone.

"We'll make it," Matt assured her, but his words carried no conviction. The rawhiders held all of the high cards, and Cud Hooker would know exactly how best to play them.

"What's it like back where you came from?" he asked, loosening his shirt. Perhaps if he talked about something she was familiar with it would lessen her fear.

"Nothing like this. We have lots of trees—big ones—and there's grass everywhere, and plenty of water. It's cool, and there are people all around, I don't mean just on the streets but out in the country."

"This country's settling fast, be just like that someday," Matt said. "And far as trees and grass go, there's plenty of both in some parts, specially along the rivers and in the valleys. Not all of it is desert."

"Most of what I've seen has been," Holly said, following his example and loosening some of her clothing. "It all seems like a wasteland. I don't see how even the wild animals survive."

"They do, and the folks who settle and start cattle ranches or homesteads make it. It's a hard life, sure, and they knew it would be at the start, so they expected it. But they find the independence they're looking for and they don't ever have to buckle down to anybody."

"Is it always this hot? Isn't there ever any snow or rain?"

"Sure, when the season's right. And the snow can get pretty deep in some parts in the winter. Expect you have hard winters back in Pennsylvania now and then."

"Yes, it does happen—ever so often."

Movement in the clean, burning sky far overhead caught Matt's attention. Buzzards. Several of them soaring gracefully in a broad circle off to the right of the *malpaís*. It was a grim omen—but he'd not call the girl's attention to the big scavengers. It would only upset her further.

"Same goes for out here—and you've got to understand that the country's not all like this. We're in the high plains. We have green valleys and grassy flats, and plenty of trees same as you do. You just ain't seen that part yet."

"I suppose you're right," Holly murmured, manner more composed as she dabbed at her face and neck with a handkerchief. Dark, damp spots showed in several places on her checked shirt, and there was a ruddiness to her skin from the relentless heat.

"But I don't think I could ever grow accustomed to living out here," she continued. "I'd always be remembering how Papa and Mama died, and what I went through—still am in fact. Matt, if we come out of this alive, will you drive me to some town—I don't care which—where I can get a stagecoach or a train to back East? I'm asking you—not trying to force you."

She had called him by name, and despite the critical situation they were in, the hammering heat, it sounded good and brought a smile to his cracked lips.

"Sure. Was what I aimed to do all along. Was just having trouble making you listen to me."

"I'm sorry about that," Holly said contritely, "but I was so upset about my parents, and then there were those horrible men—rawhiders you called them—and I thought you were one of them; I guess I just couldn't think straight."

"Was a bad time for you all right," Matt said, eyes fixed on the mound of rock and weeds behind which Hooker and Drumm had hidden. He thought he had seen movement on the part of one of them but it proved to be only a lizard.

How much longer was Hooker going to stall? Would he wait until noon, hoping the heat would drive Holly and him out into the open? That could come to pass. The girl was already suffering and thirst was beginning to be a problem for them both.

In their haste to leave the wagon there had been no time to snatch up one of the buckets and fill it from the keg.

"Gets much hotter I'm going to have to chance making it to the wagon and getting us some water," Buckman said, shifting about. His shirt was plastered to his body, and inside his boots it felt as if there were fire. "We can't stand this much longer."

"They'll see you," Holly said worriedly, and broke off abruptly when Matt lifted a hand for silence.

He thought he had heard a faint jingling—the same as Rooster's big Mexican spurs made. But the sound had come from somewhere in the rocks and scrubby growth behind them. The rawhiders couldn't have possibly circled around to their rear without his having seen them, Matt was certain—unless they had crawled belly-flat over the hot ground.

"Did you hear something?" Holly asked.

"Thought maybe I did," Buckman replied, and then, as the dry scrape of a bootheel on the rough surface of a lava rock came to him, he whirled.

Rooster Drumm, crouched in a stand of tall weeds, was drawing his pistol. Apparently he had come upon Matt and the girl sooner than expected, for his face showed surprise.

Matt brought up his gun fast and fired. Rooster yelled as the bullet drove into him, rocked him to his heels. Reflex action caused him to trigger his own weapon as he began to fall. Buckman heard the bullet strike a rock near where Holly crouched. The girl cried out in alarm as the slug screamed off into space—but there was no chance to see if she had been hurt. The dark, looming bulk of Cud Hooker was lunging at him from the opposite side of the mound.

Matt pivoted, whipped up his pistol to fire point-blank at the set, grimy face of the rawhider. He was too close. Hooker lashed out with a balled fist, knocked the weapon from Buckman's hand, and sent it flying off into the rocks. Frantic, Matt threw himself to one side to avoid the knife Hooker held in his other hand. The blade missed by only an inch, clicked metallically as it glanced off a bit of lava, while Matt, rolling away, tried to locate and recover his gun.

Cursing, Hooker hurried in between Matt and the girl, knife glittering in one hand, thick fingers of the other outspread as he sought to seize Buckman and pin him down so that he could use the blade.

Lunging to his feet Buckman began to back away. He had failed to locate his gun, but somewhere behind him would be Rooster Drumm's. If he could get to it he'd have a chance. Abruptly Matt went over backward, his heel catching against a rock. He hit flat, head striking solid surface. It stunned him for only a fragment of time, the knowledge that death was closing in on him sharpening his senses. Again rolling to one side he came up hard against one of the larger rocks. Desperate, he reversed his movement, struggled to pull away. All motion stopped as Hooker's booted foot came down on his chest and pressed him to the ground.

"My turn now, you double-crossing, lying bastard!" the big rawhider shouted.

Matt saw Cud's arm go up, saw the bright flash of sunlight on the poised blade. The sharp crack of a pistol suddenly sent echoes rolling across the *mal-país*. Hooker stiffened. A strange look came into his eyes, and twisting slowly about he stared at Holly Gannon. Smoke drifted lazily about her as she stood, half crouched, Matt Buckman's .45 clutched in her two hands, cocked and ready to fire again. The rawhider hung there motionless for a long breath, silhouetted against the hot, cloudless sky, and then toppled, his thick body falling across Buckman's.

20

Matt rolled Hooker's body aside and, breathing hard, sat up. He glanced at Holly Gannon. The girl was on her knees, the pistol still clutched tightly in her two hands. She seemed in a daze, her eyes fixed on the lifeless bulk of the rawhider.

That she had been able to summon enough courage to kill a man, feeling as he knew she did about it, was beyond understanding—a miracle, one Buckman was grateful for. He would be a dead man at that very moment otherwise, as he would never have been able to ward off the sharp blade that Hooker, probably twice his weight and double his strength, was about to plunge into him.

Sweat-soaked, bits of leaves, twigs, and dirt clinging to him, Matt got to his feet and crossed to the girl. Putting an arm about her he gently took the .45 from her hands and slid it into its holster.

"Everything's all right," he said quietly. "It's all over."

Holly looked at him and suddenly began to weep. "I—I've killed a man," she said brokenly.

"He wasn't a man—wasn't even a poor excuse," Buckman said. "He was nothing."

"But I shot—killed him."

"I'm mighty glad of that," Matt said with a wry

smile. "Anyway, you had no choice. If he'd stuck that big toad-stabber of his into me, I'd be a goner, and he'd had what he wanted all along—you. It's best you shot him to keep that from happening."

Holly ceased her crying and began to dab at her eyes with a handkerchief. "I just can't believe it," she murmured. "I've never killed anything—not even a rabbit; now I've killed a man. This country! Oh, this terrible, wild country, it does things to a person, horrible things. I don't know if—"

"You can't judge the country by what went on here. Not many men running loose like Cud Hooker and his bunch. They're a different breed—the lawless kind. You won't come up against them often, maybe not even once in a lifetime. You had the bad luck of meeting them first off. . . . You want a drink of water?"

Holly nodded and, as Matt straightened up his lank shape, allowed him to help her to her feet also. He hesitated, looked at Rooster Drumm's crumpled body lying among the burning rocks.

"Expect I best see if he's dead first," he said matter-of-factly, and moved to the side of the young rawhider.

There was no need for a close examination. The bullet from Matt's .45 had driven into Rooster's chest, probably killing him instantly. Buckman, crouched beside the man, felt a passing wave of pity and regret for him. Of the rawhiders he was the best of all—but he was one of them, with the same thoughts, the same desires as Cud Hooker and Fargo Smith. Had he lived and had his way he would do the same as his partners.

Reaching down Matt unbuckled Rooster's gun-belt and holster, pulled them free of the body, and retrieving the pistol which lay nearby rolled them into a bundle and started back to where Holly was waiting. He didn't want the rawhider's weapon and belt as a trophy and didn't need it for his own use; it was that he was observing the unwritten law to never leave firearms around for Indians to find.

Holly was walking slowly toward the wagon when he rejoined her, and together they continued on through the driving heat to where the vehicle stood. Tossing Rooster's gear into the bed of the wagon, Matt drew a tin dipper of water from the keg and handed it to the girl. While she drank he took time to also fill the feed buckets and treated each of the horses to a little water. That done Matt slaked his own thirst and, helping the girl up onto the seat of the vehicle, pulled himself to her side.

"Reckon we're ready to head on west," he said. "Can chance going the other way—back to this Edom—if you want. Could be those renegade Kiowas've moved on—"

"No, let's do like you want. I can leave from Santa Fe just as easily as I can from Edom."

"Maybe we won't have to go that far. There's some towns in between here and there where you might make arrangements to sell off your rig, and catch a stage east."

Holly, fully composed now, shrugged. "I hope so. And I wish I had Papa's money. It would simplify things so."

Matt, in the act of reaching for the lines, drew back. The money. He'd intended to search Hooker's body for it in the event that Cud, finding the cash when he went through the Gannon wagon and not wanting to share it with his partners, as Holly had suggested, had it concealed on his person.

"Be back in a couple of minutes," Buckman said, and dropping to the ground returned to where the rawhiders lay.

There was no money on Hooker, none on Rooster Drumm—which was to be expected. And there was no way of learning for sure if Fargo Smith had it other than returning to the grove and going through his clothing. But it was not likely Fargo would have the money; Cud Hooker was first in everything—even when it came to searching through the Gannon wagon.

Retracing his steps Matt climbed up onto the seat beside the girl. "No luck," he said.

Holly settled back, disappointment again having its depressing way with her. "I've been hoping against hope all along that we'd find it," she murmured. "Seems now I'd better make up my mind to forget about it."

Matt, taking the sideways position on the seat that he had adopted in the interest of comfort, gathered up the leathers and put the team into motion. He would have liked to say something comforting to the girl but could think of nothing as he pointed the team for the trail.

After a bit she turned, looked back toward the *malpaís*. "Shouldn't we bury them—those two men? After all they were human beings," she said. The amenities of the civilization she was accustomed to were still dominant in her attitude.

"Be hard to do. That's all lava rock—hard as iron. We couldn't dig a grave if we tried all day. Best to just let—"

Matt broke off as the wagon's left front wheel struck a rock and jolted vigorously. He cast a sidelong glance at her. Holly was staring at him, her pale blue eyes filled with concern.

"You mean just let the animals—the vultures—take care of them?"

Buckman nodded. "That's the way it has to be out here sometimes. Don't always have a choice."

Holly sighed and, hands folded in her lap, settled back wearily. "I could never get used to the way things are out here—not in a thousand years. I know I've said it before—and I really do mean it."

"It'll all change," Buckman said. "Time will come when it'll be just like where you came from. What will you do when you get back there to this—this—"

"Carlisle," Holly said, supplying the name of her hometown. "I don't know. I'll just have to wait and see."

"If it's anything like out here there's not many jobs a woman can do—work in a saloon maybe unless she's got the money to go into business for herself—a dressmaker's shop, something like that."

"It's some different back home. I might be able to get on as a librarian, or perhaps clerk in a store that sells ladies' clothing. What I would like to do is become a teacher."

They were almost to the trail and the point where Matt would swing the team west and begin the long journey to Santa Fe.

"What about you?" Holly asked. "You've never

talked about yourself much. Are you married? Do you have a family around somewhere?"

"Answer's no both times. Lost my folks up Kansas way in an Indian raid years ago, and when it comes to taking a wife, I reckon I'm not ready yet."

"Not ready? You must be at least in your mid-twenties."

"Not what I mean. It's that I'm not ready to quit my kind of life—cowpunching, taking off when the work's done, going to town and having myself a time with nobody telling me what I can do—or depending on me for anything."

"No woman, that's what you're saying—"

"Reckon so. Whatever, I like being without any strings tied to me, and just being able to do what I take a notion to do. Just like catching me a ride to Chicago with some rancher and his herd. If I had a family I couldn't do that."

"No, I suppose not," Holly Gannon said. "But I can't help thinking about all that you miss—a home, people who love you, and having a son or a daughter who'll look up to you."

Buckman's shoulders stirred. "Everything's got a price. A man pays for whatever he does in some way. . . . Here's where we start heading west."

At once Holly laid a hand on his arm. "Would it be too much trouble to find the rawhiders' wagon? I'd like to get back the things they took—the silverware and jewelry, and there are some pictures. They're all I'll have to remember the family by."

"Sure," Matt said, and cutting the dun team around headed into the grove.

The wagon should be somewhere near. Hooker

had abandoned it shortly after Fargo Smith had been shot out of the saddle, at which time the big rawhider took possession of his partner's horse.

"Maybe when we reach Santa Fe there'll still be time enough for you to catch a stagecoach to Dodge City and get that job with the rancher who's shipping his cattle to Chicago—"

"Doubt it; Santa Fe's a far piece. But it don't matter—if I can't make it this year maybe I can next."

Holly sighed, brushed at the perspiration on her face with a handkerchief. "I just wish we'd found Papa's money. Then I could pay you for helping me—"

A deep frown crossed Matt Buckman's sun-browned features. Hauling back on the lines he drew the horses to a stop. Holly turned to him in alarm.

"What is it, Matt? Is there something wrong?"

"Your saying something about driving sort of jabbed me," Buckman replied, wrapping the leathers around the whip handle. "This seat's not a comfortable one—too low. Makes my knees stick up high."

"Papa was a short man—"

"Know that, and I figured that was why the seat was fixed like it is. He changed it, made it lower to the floorboards—and maybe he didn't! Maybe it's the floor that's higher, not the seat lower."

Holly was leaning forward with him, both staring at the boards beneath their feet.

"Do you think Papa could have—"

"He didn't put a false bottom in the wagon bed,

probably because that's an old trick, but up front under his feet he maybe used the same idea."

Matt turned, dropped to the ground, and obtained the ax secured in a metal bracket on the side of the vehicle. Coming about hurriedly, he climbed up onto the seat.

"It's sure worth a look," he said in a taut voice. "Your pa might've fixed himself a place to hide his money where he figured nobody would ever think to look."

21

The ax blade was too thick. After endeavoring to wedge it under the top floorboard, Matt laid the tool aside and glanced into the back of the wagon.

Holly, her eyes bright with hope and excitement, looked at him anxiously. "What's the matter? Don't you think there's—"

"Need something smaller than the ax, something I can work with," Buckman answered. "Your pa, being a hardware man, is bound to have some tools along."

"Here, behind the seat," the girl said as Matt started to crawl over into the bed of the wagon and search among the articles, "there's a toolbox. I've seen him put things in there—a hammer and saw and the like—many times."

Matt said nothing, and crawling over the back of the seat he knelt in front of the hinged and hasped box extending the width of the bed. It had been opened, he saw, probably by Cud Hooker or Fargo Smith when they ransacked the vehicle for the money they were certain Caleb Gannon had with him. Lifting the lid Buckman removed a hammer and a two-inch wood chisel.

"This ought to do it," he said, climbing back into the front.

Leaning over, Matt wedged the sharp blade under the top board of what now at closer inspection looked to be a boxlike arrangement and gave the tool a solid blow with the hammer. The nails holding the strip of lumber gave. Laying the hammer aside, Matt pried up. The top board came readily, and pushing it back he grinned at Holly.

"Looks like we drew an ace," he said.

The girl, eyes wide, lips parted in a combination of surprise, relief, and delight, smiled back at him. "I—I don't know what to say—whether to laugh or cry!"

Matt picked up one of the several canvas bags. Untying the string he withdrew from it a thick fold of currency. "Quite a few dollars here—a thousand at least."

Passing it to Holly he examined the remaining sacks. Some contained more paper money, others were heavy with gold eagles and silver dollars.

"There's so much!" Holly marveled. "I never realized Papa had all this—"

"You can do anything you want now—go back to Pennsylvania and start living the kind of life you want," Buckman said as he opened a leather folder thick with legal-appearing papers and documents. He studied them briefly and again glanced at the girl.

"Seems you've got some property in some town called Wickenburg—in Arizona. Deed's right here. Your pa must have made a deal before you pulled out."

"I remember Papa having some business with a man who sold real estate," Holly said, "but I assumed it had to do with selling the hardware store. I never thought about him buying us a home ahead of time."

"Expect he wanted to have a place all ready to move into when you got there," Matt said, starting to return the papers and the sacks to the box. "I think we'd best nail this back together until we get to where we're going."

Smiling happily, Holly nodded. "But I'll be needing a little cash for supplies along the way," she said, extracting several eagles and silver dollars from the canvas bag she still held, and thrusting them into her pocket. "Oh, this is so wonderful—I owe you so much, Matt!"

He shrugged as she handed the bank sack to him. "You don't owe me nothing. We both just got caught in the same trap—Hooker and them. I'm mighty glad it all worked out," he said, nailing the lid of the box into place.

"It was smart of you to guess where he hid the money," Holly said as he replaced the tools in the chest.

"Was my aching legs that gave me the idea—not my being smart," Buckman said with a laugh as he took up the lines. "The real smart one was your pa. Plenty of pilgrims build a false bottom in their wagon to hide valuables. It's about the first place men like Hooker and Fargo Smith will look. False floorboards is a new idea."

"Thanks to him being a short man!" Holly said. She was in high, good spirits. Her cheeks were glowing and there was a bright sparkle in her eyes.

Buckman lifted the reins, started to put the team

in motion. The girl checked him by grasping the leathers with her hand. He turned to her questioningly.

"Something wrong?"

The sun was bearing down with its full force now and while it was not as hot in the grove as it had been in the *malpaís* the heat was making itself felt.

"Finding the money changes everything," she said, leaning back and dabbing at the moisture on her face with the bit of lace-edged cloth. "I think now I'll go on to Wickenburg. I'm sure that's what my folks would want me to do. There's really no reason to go back to Carlisle."

"Got it in mind that you wanted to get out of this country fast as you could—"

"I did—at first—but like I say the money changes everything. For one thing I have a home now—in this place called Wickenburg. Do you know anything about the town?"

"Never been there—not even much in Arizona. Heard it's a lot like around here."

"It was once all New Mexico, but some army general during the war divided it and declared the western half a new territory. They called it Arizona."

"Didn't know about that," Matt said. "Got to be fine country if that's how it is. Sure don't see how you could make a mistake by going on to there."

Holly faced him squarely. "I can forget Pennsylvania in time—and with a little help. Matt, would you be willing to go on with me—drive me to Wickenburg?"

Buckman shifted the lines to his left hand, rubbed

at his whisker-stubbled jaw with the other. "Well. I ain't so anxious to move on—"

"You need a job," Holly said, hurriedly pointing out the fact to him, "and you lost your horse and all of your belongings when the Indians attacked you. And you've already missed your chance to go to Chicago."

Buckman nodded. "Expect you're right all the way."

"I'd pay you, of course, just hire you on as a driver. I can't do it alone, and I'd be afraid to hire on some stranger."

Matt said nothing, just let the girl's words hang in the hot, still air.

"You could come back here to your part of New Mexico if you didn't like it in Wickenburg—but I'd like it if you'd stay. I—I think I've fallen in love with you, Matt."

Buckman, staring straight ahead, stirred uncomfortably. He had found himself feeling much the same toward Holly Gannon but had steadfastly resisted it. He wasn't ready to settle down; there were still many places he wanted to go, to see, and besides he liked the free if sometimes hard life of a working cowhand. That it would be wonderful to have a beautiful wife like Holly was undeniable—but it just wasn't time yet to marry and settle down. He rubbed at his jaw again, seeking the proper words, knowing he must say something.

"I'm right proud to hear you think that much of me, but I ain't sure it would work—"

"Why not?"

"Well, for one thing I'm just a cowboy while

you're a real pretty woman with a lot of education—
and money. I'm not sure we'd fit together."

Holly, fanning herself with the handkerchief,
looked away. "I think you're wrong," she murmured.

"Sure wouldn't be the first time," Matt said, and
put the team into movement. "I'll drive you to
Wickenburg, but about the other—well, we'll just
have to do a bit more thinking and talking about—"

Holly suddenly halted his words by raising her
arm and pointing ahead. "There's the wagon," she
said.

Buckman followed the line of her leveled finger.
The rig was standing off in the thick brush well back
from the trail. Barely visible, it had not moved far
from where he expected to find it. A saddle horse,
the one he had ridden and that had belonged to
Penmon was nearby.

At once Matt veered the duns toward the abandoned vehicle. Once Holly's property was recovered he'd unhitch the team pulling the rawhider's
wagon so they would be free to forage for themselves. It wouldn't be right to leave them there har-
nessed to the vehicle. He wished now he had taken
time to do something about the two other saddle
horses—the ones that Cud Hooker and Rooster
Drumm had been riding. They would still be standing patiently at the edge of the *malpais* where the
two men had left them. Maybe, when Holly was
through collecting the items from the wagon that
she wanted, he'd circle back to the lava beds before
heading on west and bring the horses to the grove

where they could also graze until someone came along and claimed them.

Abruptly the duns came to a startled halt. A figure, bloody and disheveled, had stepped out from behind a clump of oak to the left. A leveled pistol was in his hand. It took but one glance for Matt to recognize the man: Fargo Smith.

22

A scream burst from Holly Gannon's lips. "I—I thought he was dead!" she cried in a shocked voice. "How—"

Matt scarcely heard her. He was as surprised as the girl, had believed the rawhider was out of this life for good, as were Cud Hooker and Rooster Drumm.

But he was wrong: Fargo was very much alive. The bullet that had been fired at him, in haste, apparently had struck the outlaw in the upper arm and passing on through, grazed his head and knocked him unconscious from his horse. That he had lost much blood was evident but it seemed not to be hindering much. Eyes glittering with hate, bearded jaw set, he motioned with the gun menacingly.

"Climb down, you goddamn double-dealing sonofabitch! I'm going to blow your head off!"

Matt considered his options. There were none. He was a dead man if he did as Fargo Smith ordered, was equally dead if he did not.

Leaning forward slowly Matt wrapped the lines about the whipstock. He could think of only one thing to do if he was to save Holly and himself: suddenly throw himself off the wagon at Fargo.

Maybe Smith, taken by surprise, would trigger his weapon too fast and the bullet would miss its intended target. If it did, Buckman felt he would at least have a chance. Coming back around he stared at Fargo as he gathered his legs under him and prepared to launch himself at the outlaw.

The gold watch chain that Fargo wore looped across his belly now dangled loosely from one vest pocket. Dark bloodstains crusted his yellow shirt, and he had used his neckerchief as bandage for the wound in his arm. Bits of leaves and other debris clung to his dusty clothing, and dark soil was plastered to the left side of his face.

"Was about to climb on Penmon's horse and come after you," Fargo said in a low voice. "Aimed to track you down if it took till doomsday—then I seen you. You getting down or am I shooting you off'n that seat? Would do it anyhow only I ain't chancing hurting the little gal."

"I'm climbing down," Matt said, rising slowly.

"I reckon you done something to Cud and Rooster, maybe shot them in the back when they wasn't looking—"

"They're dead sure enough," Buckman replied, and putting all his strength into it, literally threw himself at the outlaw.

In that same fraction of time he heard Holly Gannon scream, realized that she had done so in hopes of distracting Fargo. It had the desired effect. The rawhider's agate-hard eyes shifted only momentarily to the girl but long enough to destroy his concentration. He fired his weapon. Matt felt the breath of the bullet as it grazed his cheek, and then came the solid impact of the collision with Fargo.

They went down together, Smith on the bottom. Matt struggled to draw his .45 and regain his feet but Fargo, strong as a grizzly and amazingly fast for so big a man, knocked Matt aside, rolled away, and bounded upright.

"Now, you lousy backstabber," he yelled, bringing up his gun, "I—"

Matt, pistol out and partly hidden by his own sprawling body, fired quickly. The bullet drove into the big outlaw's chest, caused him to stagger, fall back a step. Still on his feet, he raised his weapon again. Buckman triggered a second shot. Fargo Smith paused. Both arms sank slowly to his sides as an angry frown distorted his face. His stiffening fingers straightened, released the pistol he was holding, and allowed it to drop, and then abruptly he crumpled.

Holly was off the wagon immediately. She ran to Matt, anxiously looked up at him. "Are you hurt? Did he shoot you?"

Matt shook his head. "Got lucky—it was close, but he missed," he said, grinning in relief. "Like somebody once said, there ain't nothing like the good feeling a man gets when somebody shoots at him and misses."

Holly laughed at his humor, impulsively threw her arms about him. "Oh, I'm so glad, Matt! I was afraid—"

"That yelling you did sure helped," he said, putting his arms about her. It felt good, holding her close. "Owe you for that. It sort of threw him off enough—"

Matt broke off. Standing beside his horse in the brush near the wagon was U.S. Deputy Marshal John Wingert. The lawman, gun in hand, was eyeing them coldly. Releasing Holly, Buckman stepped back.

"What's going on here?" Wingert demanded, walking forward slowly. "What was that shooting?"

Matt pointed at Fargo Smith's slack figure. "Was between him and me."

"Looks like you were faster."

"Maybe just luckier," Matt said.

Wingert glanced about. "Where's the rest of your bunch—Hooker and whatever it was the other one was called?"

"You'll find them dead over in the *malpais.*"

Wingert pushed his too-large hat to the back of his head, his dark eyes narrowing. "Maybe you best drop that six-shooter," he said, and when Matt complied, added: "You kill them?"

Matt hesitated only briefly, and then nodded. "Yeh, reckon I did. Was them or me—just like it was with Fargo."

"You were one of them. What did you do—decide to take over the outfit for yourself?"

"I never was one of them, Marshal," Buckman said, and gave his explanation of how he happened to be with the rawhiders. "Day you rode in I was hoping to get a word with you, tell you what was going on, but I never got the chance."

Wingert shrugged. "That's you talking. Seems to me you were hand-in-glove with them."

"Maybe looked that way to you, but I wasn't. And I couldn't do anything that day but keep my mouth shut. All the time you were there Fargo Smith was holding a gun on you."

The lawman considered Buckman's words for a time. Then, "Could be you're telling me the truth—and it could be you ain't. If the rest of the rawhiders—"

"Rawhiding wasn't all they were doing," Matt broke in. "If you'll take a look in their wagon you'll find plenty of stuff they took off the pilgrims they held up—and murdered."

"We're all pretty sure that was a bunch of renegade Kiowas or Comanches—"

"They made it look like it by throwing arrows around and burning the wagons."

"You in on that, too—the robbing and the killings?"

"I was there," Matt admitted, "but I kept out of it—the killing part. Just helped with the burying and setting fire to the wagons. I—"

"What Matt is telling you is all true, Marshal," Holly said, coming into the conversation. "I know because they murdered my parents and would have killed me, too, if it hadn't been for him. He got me away from them, then had to fight them all to keep us both alive. He's not one of them, Marshal, and never was."

Wingert shrugged, holstered his pistol, and reaching up removed his hat. Taking his neckerchief, he mopped at the sweat on his face.

"Well, seems I'll just have to believe you. Seems logical, anyway. You don't look like any rawhider

I've ever seen," Wingert said, nodding to Matt, and then, looking at Holly Gannon, added: "And you, young lady, you're obviously real quality. I can't figure you cooking up a lie like that for him."

"You've been told gospel," Buckman said. "But if you want, we can ride back to the ranch where I've been working. Foreman there'll tell you who I am and that I ain't no rawhider."

"Won't be necessary," Wingert said briskly, moving up to Fargo Smith and picking up the outlaw's gun. Thrusting it under his belt he turned back to Matt. "I'll be obliged if you'll get a shovel and help me bury this man. Others over in the *malpaís,* well, I expect they've already been taken care of."

Buckman recovered his .45, crossed to the Gannon wagon, and obtaining the necessary tool began to hollow out a trench alongside Smith's body. Holly, as if repelled by the sight, turned away to stare out over the blistered plain.

Shortly Wingert relieved Matt of the task and completed the digging, after which, together, they rolled the outlaw into the shallow grave and covered it over.

"Best we can do for him—and considering all the killing he's had a hand in, it's more than he deserves," the lawman said. "Sure obliged to you for your help."

Matt shrugged. "No thanks needed. Will you be taking their wagon on with you?"

"Only thing I can do—but I sure ain't looking forward to it: the stink's curling my nose clear over here. I'll head for the closest town—there's a settlement north of here a ways—and turn the rig over to

P010

the sheriff there, and let him take care of the stuff you say is in it."

"It's there, all right, hid under the hides. You say you're going north. That'll take you by the *malpaís*. You'll find the horses Hooker and Rooster were riding there. I'd be obliged if you'd add them to your string and take them on with the wagon and the sorrel standing next to it."

"Sure—no trouble."

"About the stuff in Hooker's wagon, there's one sack that belongs to the lady. It be all right if I get it for her?"

"If it's hers she's got a right to it," the lawman said. "Which way will you be going?"

"On west, to some town in Arizona Territory called Wickenburg," Matt replied. "Aim to ask the lady to be my wife when we get there. Decided I've done enough fiddle-footing."

"Sounds like you're doing the smart thing," Wingert said. "Good luck."

Matt Buckman scarcely heard the lawman's words. His attention was on Holly. She had wheeled, was hurrying toward him, eyes bright, a smile on her lips.

About the Author

Ray Hogan is the author of more than one hundred books and two hundred articles and short stories. His father was an early Western marshal, and Hogan himself has spent a lifetime researching the West firsthand from his home in Albuquerque, New Mexico. His work has been filmed, televised, and translated into eighteen languages. His most recent novels are *The Doomsday Canyon, The Vengeance of Fortuna West, The Renegade Gun,* and *The Doomsday Bullet.*